GUNSHY

By Louise Titchener

Prologue

Baltimore 1882

T he Capital Express shuddered to a halt. Ben Magruder squinted out the window.
"Why are we stopping?"

"Carrolton Viaduct," said Enoch Rubman. "Most likely a freight barring our way. Give it a few minutes and we'll be rolling again."

Ira Nutwell studied his cards. "You ought to know, being as you're the big railroad man. By the way, the whores in D.C. were right accommodating. How'd you know about that house?"

"Research. Nothing but the best for old soldiers." Enoch puffed on his cigar and smiled lazily.

A half an hour earlier the three men had finished an eight-course dinner inside the train's luxurious private car. Now its curtains of plum velvet shielded the three of them from the fireflies flickering in the soft Maryland night. The glow shed by the car's batwing gas burners burnished their faces. Their eyes glistened with memories.

Nutwell stroked his luxurious auburn mustache. "You ever think about that cave, Enoch?"

"Never. That's the past."

"Past has a way of coming back at you."

"Not when you've got my future."

Nutwell guffawed. "Damn, but who would have thought it!" He punched Enoch's shoulder. "You such a big muckety muck with the B&O. You the worst hellraiser of the bunch! Now you're a family man."

"Two kiddies and another in the oven," Rubman agreed. He chewed his cigar with enjoyment. "The wife is just what she should be. Reads the Bible and thinks of nothing but good works." He winked at Magruder. The thin, balding man with the goatee winked back, then looked around frowning. "What the devil?"

The train's iron wheels had been silent for several minutes. Now a loud clacking became a thunderous roar.

"Christ!" Enoch leaped to his feet, knocking back his seat. The bottle of very old rye the men had been slowly draining crashed to the floor amidst scattered cards. While his friends cursed, Enoch dashed to the rear window and tore aside a curtain. His insides liquefied. "Run for it. We're being telescoped!"

Nutwell and Magruder were out of their seats, Enoch well ahead of them. He knew about telescoped railroad cars. He'd seen the splintered wood and twisted metal, the burned and broken bodies. Escape! But he was too late. The runaway car he'd spied coming at them plunged through the rear of the private car like a brick through a cracker box. Ripping wood howled and tortured metal shrieked. The private car was up-ended and shoved overtop the one ahead. Seconds later it exploded into flames with the three men trapped inside.

CHAPTER ONE

Deputy Marshal Rackley spit a brown wad onto the wood floor. "Time to see if you're as good as you're cracked up." His voice dripped doubt.

Oliver Redcastle folded his jacket over the back of a chair stacked with ladies undergarments. He knocked a stack of corsets off another chair and positioned it at an angle to the window. He took the Remington-Beals Single Shot out of its deer hide case. It's curly maple stock, well-polished by years of use, glowed in the dim light.

He ran a finger down its barrel to check its convertible front site, then peered through the rear site. He manipulated its action to assure himself that it was still smooth as cold satin. It was. He slid in a .32 rimfire cartridge. With an effort, because his knee had been paining him all day, he knelt in front of the open window and rested his bent elbow on the edge of the chair. Slowly, he leaned his weight on it and began working the rifle's butt into his shoulder.

Rackley and Lieutenant Krooth of the Eastern District had commandeered this third floor bedroom atop a corset shop opposite Hiram Flatt's tin emporium. Flatt was holed up with an eight-year-old girl he'd kidnapped hours earlier.

Since two other city children of a similar age had been kidnapped, molested and murdered recently, the Baltimore police assumed Flatt intended the same fate for his present victim. This time, however, the tin man had made an error.

The other two hapless children had been the offspring of immigrant cannery workers. The police had not exerted themselves. This child, Annie Bailey, was the pampered daughter of a prominent banker. Soon after she'd disappeared, lawmen scoured the city. Now, they'd cordoned off the cobblestone block on either side of Flatt's house. Around the barriers neigbors and curiosity seekers pressed against the officers grimly standing guard in the dusk.

"Light's mighty poor. Think you can get him, Redcastle?"

"Depends if he shows himself at the window before dark. If he stays out of sight, you may have to rush the house." Oliver passed a hand over his forehead. If Flatt didn't show himself, he might be harming the child. If, on the other hand, the tinsmith did show himself Oliver would have to kill him. He'd hoped he wouldn't have to kill a man again.

Rackley tugged at his muttonchop whiskers, then took another cut of tobacco and thrust it into the corner of his mouth. He was beefy, with a ruddy complexion that suggested a quick temper. "Flatt's a cornered rat," he said between chews. "If we rush him, he'll kill the child. Lord knows what he's done to the poor kiddie already. I know her father."

Oliver understood what it meant to be a father with a child at risk. He shifted some of his weight off his right elbow. Concentration was everything these situations. Let your mind wander and you'd lose your chance. Nevertheless, it was a chore to ignore Rackley spitting as his square-toed shoes paced a groove in the floor.

Rackley said, "I only made such fuss to get you here because my man, Gloger, is down sick. Gloger's the best shot in fifty miles."

"That so?"

"During the war he went sesesh. Shot blue coats out of the trees like ripe fruit."

Oliver wished Rackley would shut up. The reek coming off him suggested that his monthly bath was inadequate.

"How'd you get to be a marksman, Redcastle?"

"Shooting rattlesnakes for dinner."

"Ain't no rattlesnakes in Baltimore."

I grew up in Kansas." He let his gaze flicker over the street below. Flatt appeared to be quite an accomplished tinsmith.

His shop windows were stuffed with pans, kettles, buckets, squirrel cages and the small tin horns used by garbage cart drivers and fish peddlers.

Some of the neighbors shouting jeers at Flatt's upper windows had doubtless patronized his business never guessing his sick obsession with children.

"If I get a clear shot at him," Oliver said, "do you want me to wing him?"

"Don't take chances. Do whatever need be to save the child."

"It may already be too late for that."

Across the street an unseen hand shoved up a window. The grimy strip of burlap covering it was torn aside and the silhouette of a smallish man appeared. In front of him was the child. Flatt pressed a knife to Annie Bailey's throat and held her close to shield himself.

A cry went up from the crowd outside the cordon of police. As Oliver squinted down the Remington's long barrel, he heard it only as a muted roar, like the rush of waves on a distant shore.

It was that twilight period when solid shapes dissolve into shadow and dusk deceives the eye. But Oliver saw Flatt as if the man were bathed in radiance. The universe contained only himself, Flatt, and the child between them. Time slowed to the heavy tick of his pulse.

Crack.

Horrified screams wavered up from the crowd. The knife dropped away from little Annie Bailey's throat. Behind her, Flatt swayed and jerked. Slowly, he sagged out of sight. A bullet hole divided his colorless eyebrows.

CHAPTER TWO

Two hours later Oliver climbed off a horse-drawn streetcar. He adjusted the weight of the Remington slung over his shoulder in its case, and set off toward home. Limping down the brick sidewalk, he passed three boys playing leapfrog. Lilac, brick dust and horse urine scented the warm night.

He'd recently inherited his aunt's red brick rowhouse. As a child he had visited her in summer and admired the handsome brass knocker on her paneled door and the white marble steps and fancy iron rail that led up to her entrance. Those features still pleased him. Yet, if it weren't for his daughter, he might have sold the place instead of moving to Baltimore to make it his home.

Inside, Mrs. Milawny eyed the Remington weighing down his shoulder. "And did everything go well, sir? It give me a turn when the police came asking after you."

Mrs. Milawny had been in Oliver's employ for less than a week. She was a pleasant, motherly woman with an aphorism for every occasion. A pouf of blinding white hair crowned her broad forehead. With her crinkled blue eyes and apple cheeks she looked a proper mate for Father Christmas. So far she and Chloe had been dealing well together. Which was a blessing since the child was still nervous of him.

"I used to be in law enforcement. The local police needed some help with a kidnap case."

"That's why you took that big gun with you tonight?" Her white eyebrows flew up. "You wouldn't be a Pinkerton man, would you?"

"I was that for many years. No more. You needn't fear I'll be dealing with crooks. I'm here in Baltimore to open a new sort of business."

"You don't say so. And what would that be, sir?"

"Don't know just yet. I've given myself a year to look around before I decide. Is Chloe asleep?"

The interest on the housekeeper's face shifted to concern. "She's having a hard time with the asthma tonight, poor little soul. We don't appreciate the air we breathe 'til it's hard to find. I sat with her until she finally fell asleep. It tore at my heart. She was asking about her mother."

Mrs. Milawny gave Oliver a look that invited explanation. Ignoring it, he locked away his Remington and ascended the staircase. A candle burned on a table in his daughter's room. The smell of camphor lay over the airless enclosure.

He threw back the curtains at the window and pulled up the sash. A puff of summer air, like a balloon on a thread of moonlight, streamed through the opening. Quietly, he lowered himself into the chair next to Chloe's bed. Through her shroud of mosquito netting, he studied her small face.

She resembled her pretty mother, he thought. The same thick auburn curls and alabaster skin. Was there anything of himself in those babyish features? Was he truly her father? Or had Marietta made a fool of him all over again?

As the child struggled for air, each of her labored breaths fluttered in the room like the wings of a trapped bird. A whitish film lay like a scale on her lips.

He thought of an icewagon he'd seen earlier and wished he had a sliver of that ice to lay against her tongue. He wrung a sponge out in the bowl of camphor water on the bedside table. Gently, he lifted the gauze canopy and wiped off her forehead and cheeks. It seemed to help. She turned her head and breathed a bit more easily.

Mrs. Milawny's stout body appeared in the doorway. She shot a disapproving glance at the open window and said, "You're wanted, sir. There's a man downstairs says he's got a job for you. Something about an accident on the railroad."

CHAPTER THREE

An hour later Oliver stood cooling his heels in John Work Garrett's mansion entry. The president of the B&O was doing a good job of putting his stolen riches on display, he thought as he looked around at the wainscoting and Italian landscapes in heavy gilt frames.

A butler led him into a deeply carpeted parlor where a stout man resembling a bulldog with sideburns sat behind an acre of fumed oak desk. This had to be Garrett. On a sofa to his right sat a tall, thin individual with the hatchet-faced demeanor of an undertaker. Oliver raised his eyebrows. John D. Rockefeller. Wherever Rockefeller went, there was trouble.

Garrett introduced himself and then his guest. "Mr. Rockefeller is in Baltimore on private business. He does not wish his presence in the city to be known. Is that clear?"

After Oliver said it was, Garrett cleared his throat. "I got your direction from the Pinkerton Agency. They informed me you had just recently moved to Baltimore to set up an investigation service." Garrett turned to Rockefeller. "Is this the man you had in mind?"

"Yes. He did some work for me in '72."

Garrett motioned Oliver to a seat next to a brass spittoon. He stayed on his feet. "I'm afraid you and Mr. Rockefeller have been misinformed. I've retired from law enforcement."

The railroad magnate and oil tycoon exchanged glances. Garrett said, "Indeed? If you don't plan to set up an investigation agency in the city, what are your plans?"

"I'm thinking of going into private business."

"Ah." Garrett tapped a folder atop his desk. "I have your file here, Redcastle. Judging from its contents and from what Mr.

Rockefeller tells me, you're an impressive fellow. Says here that during the war you were a sharpshooter for Little Mac. You couldn't have been more than a boy then."

"Sixteen."

"Those were hard times." Garrett rose and walked to the window where he stood with his hands behind his frockcoat. He said, "Heard about the railroad accident at the Carrolltown Viaduct two days past?"

Oliver had read of three men killed while drinking and playing cards in a private car. He hadn't given the newspaper story much attention. Railroad accidents were common.

Garrett went on, "The Sun described it as a mishap. Mr. Rockefeller and I think not. The chocks on that runaway coal car were deliberately knocked loose and the handbrake released. We think the intention was either sabotage or murder.

"Do you have any idea who might have been responsible?"

"None. That's why we need a man such as yourself, a man who knows how to find the truth."

Rockefeller added, "I had been scheduled to occupy the car the night of the accident. Fortunately, the day before I learned I would be detained in Washington."

Garrett said, "Since the car was available, Enoch Rubman, one of my executives, decided to ride up in it with a party of friends." He walked back to his desk. "Mr. Rockefeller is concerned that someone may have been trying to kill him and make it look like an accident. He would be interested to know who and why. As I see it, however, there are two other possibilities. One of those who died was a B&O man. Someone may have been trying to strike at the railroad through him. There may be attempts on other B&O executives. It won't be the first time."

"No," Oliver agreed. Thinking of Baltimore's violent railroad strikes in '73 and '77, he studied Rockefeller. If the ruthless old pirate feared assassination and Garrett thought he might be the next victim in a labor conspiracy, they'd both be willing to pay well for protection. Oliver shook his head. If he didn't have to lick these men's boots, why should he?

"I can't help you. I meant what I said about leaving law enforcement."

Rockefeller looked displeased. "There wouldn't be any law enforcement involved. What we want from you is information. You'd only be investigating, and we'd pay you well."

The figure he named made Oliver blink. Again, he shook his head. "I can't help you. That part of my life is over."

Rockefeller's humorless laugh rattled like dry paper. "That's not what I hear, Redcastle. According to my information, you just shot a man dead, a man named Flatt. That doesn't sound like the act of a peaceful citizen."

"I was cooperating with the police." Oliver supposed he shouldn't be surprised. Rockefeller had a network of spies everywhere he went. Still, it made him uneasy. He'd seen the oil baron in action, wiping out rivals and crushing opposition like a shark in a school of gold fish.

"You're the man I want for this job," Rockefeller declared softly. "You'll be hearing from me again."

CHAPTER FOUR

Two days later Oliver ran into an old colleague.

"Harry!"

"The great man himself!" Harry Barnett, one of William Pinkerton's key operatives out of Philadelphia, stood on the brick sidewalk grinning.

Oliver nudged Harry under an awning, narrowly avoiding a wetting from a passing street-sprinkler sending forth plumes of water from its hogshead on wheels. "What are you doing in Baltimore?"

"Waiting for you, old man. Your housekeeper told me where to smoke you out." Harry glanced at the painted sign above Oliver's head. "What were you about at a glovers?"

"Looking into a business opportunity."

"Gloves? You're thinking of selling gloves?" Harry hooted. "Ollie, old man, for the past twenty years you've been the scourge of the criminal element. Now you're going to hawk gloves to middle-aged ladies?"

"I haven't bought into the trade yet."

"All right, come off the roof. I won't comment further. Have you completed your business?"

"I'm through for the day."

"Let me spot you some lunch."

A half an hour later both men sipped from tankards at Sheehan's saloon and raw bar on Light Street. Crowded with traders from the Market Exchange, the place reeked of beer and cigar smoke. Over the hubbub, a piano tinkled out "Daisy, Give Me Your Answer True."

Harry Barnett lit a Virginia Bright and pushed the box across to Oliver who declined.

"Why are you here, Harry? I know better than to think you've looked me up for old times sake."

"Now, why wouldn't I make an effort to see an old and valued associate, lad?"

Harry removed his dove gray derby and slid a hand over his cap of pomaded hair. Harry Barnett was a jaunty little English-man who'd cultivated an Oxford accent. His brown eyes saw everything and were disturbed by nothing. He'd made a study of dressing in the latest mode. His expensive semi-cutaway jacket sported a velvet collar and a gold watch chain thick as a man's thumb. Despite his fancy accent and fashion plate appearance, however, Harry was one of the Pinkerton Agency's most dedi-cated operatives--a dead shot with a Navy Colt.

"We made pretty good pards, didn't we?" he said. "I saved your behind once when we were chasing the Renos."

"And I returned the favor when we were after the James boys. I read about Jesse's cousin shooting him in the back. I don't sup-pose you had anything to do with that?"

"Let's just say the old man was pleased to hear of it."

Harry referred to his former boss and mentor, Allan Pinker-ton. Oliver asked, "How is Allan?"

"Health is worse. You should see the letters he fires off to William every hour on the hour. It's killing him that he's had to turn the business over to his sons."

Oliver smiled. He was truly fond of Allan Pinkerton, the founder of the firm. The senior Pinkerton was as easy to please as a Russian emperor in a temper fit, but in some ways the im-perious Scot had replaced the father whom Oliver had lost in his youth. "There'll never be another Allan Pinkerton," he said with genuine regret.

"He's not lost to us yet, and I'd say William and Robert are doing well enough. The business is flourishing. Matter of fact, we've got more than we can handle."

Oliver thought of his recent encounter with Garrett and John D. Rockefeller. "So, I hear."

Harry asked with false casualness, "You wouldn't care to

reconsider and come back to the outfit, would you? You'd be welcomed with open arms. It's not easy to find men with your experience."

"I wouldn't. Now tell me why you've tracked me down. Are you on an assignment?"

"I'm on my way to a job in D.C., though I'll be spending plenty of time in Baltimore. Pinkerton has a contract to provide the security for the President's visit to the National Encampment."

Oliver nodded warily. Everybody knew that in just a few days the sixteenth National Convention of the Grand Army of the Republic would convene in Baltimore. Nearly all the public buildings, including the City Hall and the United States courthouse, had been decked out with flags and bunting. Veterans' delegations from all over the country could be seen greeting each other on street corners.

"Now Harry, you wouldn't be buying my lunch because of that railroad job I turned my back on a couple of days ago, would you?"

Harry blew a smoke ring, a skill which Oliver had watched him perfect during long hours spent guarding trains from lawless western gangs. Harry said, "Why do you think we recommended you to Garrett?"

"Since you know very well that I'm finished with law enforcement, I couldn't say."

Harry snorted. "Fellas like you and me can't quit the game. Hunting men gets into your blood."

"Speak for yourself."

"Oh, can it. This is Harry you're talking to. I've seen you trail a man. You're like a damned terrier with a rat. You won't let go."

"I've turned over a new leaf."

"In order to sell gloves?"

"Whatever business I go into, it won't make mortal enemies for me. I don't care to end my days like the old man, living in a fortress guarded around the clock."

As the piano in the next room struck up "On the Bowery,"

Harry's eyes narrowed. "This is really about that kiddie Marietta Dumont foisted on you, isn't it?"

"Chloe's mother is dead, Harry."

"Keeling over in that flu epidemic don't make her a saint. Marietta was a two-bit actress with a long string of lovers. Just because you were one of them don't mean the kid she left you is really yours."

"The age is right. Chloe is seven and Marietta and I met in Chicago eight years ago."

"Righto, she was an understudy in The Slave Girl's Dream and when the play's backer offered her the lead she walked out on you to shack up with him. Why ruin your career for a kid that could be his?"

"Her maid swore Chloe was mine."

"Maybe she was desperate to get rid of the child after Marietta died and you were the only one of her lovers she could bamboozle into taking the kid off her hands. I hate to see you made a fool of, old chum."

"Drop it, Harry. Chloe's my daughter."

Harry leaned across the table. "You've always been burdened with too much conscience, Ollie. Comes of being a Quaker preacher's son, I expect. Listen to me, friend. You're kidding yourself. You can't quit what you've been doing all these years and not expect to go barmy with boredom in a matter of weeks. I respect that you're trying to do the right thing for this child, give her a decent life and all that. But why should taking responsibility for a kid mean you change who you are?"

"And just who is it that you think I am?"

"A man valuable to the agency, one whose skills might keep the President of the United States from being assassinated."

"What?"

"You've got me right. I'm here because you turned down the B&O job. You must be crazy to walk out on John D. Rockefeller. He's not a man fellas like you and me turn up their noses at."

"Rockefeller is as big a crook as any of the James boys were. He just knows how to rob legally. He can hire someone else to save his thieving hide."

"Rockefeller's hide may not be the one in question. Hear me out! All three of the men fried in that so-called railroad accident Garrett told you about were Union officers. In just a few days thousands of veterans from both sides will flood this city. Many of them traveling by train."

Oliver nodded. "I see why Garrett's nervous about sabotage. A lucky strike could wipe out a car full of veterans, and that would be bad for ticket sales."

"Veterans will not be the B&O's only passengers," Barnett countered. "President Arthur, accompanied by the Secretary of State, the Secretary of War, the Attorney General and the Speaker of the House, will come into Camden Station on a rail-car furnished by the B&O at 11:00 on the 22nd of June. See where my thoughts are tending?"

"You don't really think Garrett's accident might have been part of a larger conspiracy against the President, do you?" Oliver considered this far-fetched. More than likely, whoever had set off that runaway car had done so out of some personal grudge against Rockefeller or wanted to make trouble for the railroad. If the President were the target, why alert his protectors with such a piddling preliminary strike?

"It's not what I think, it's what Allan Pinkerton thinks," Harry countered. "He's been lobbing telegrams at the office about this matter, and they've been going off on his son's desk like stinkbombs. You know how the old man's never forgiven himself because he wasn't on the job the night Lincoln was shot."

Oliver nodded. A city policeman with a "drunk and dis-orderly" record had been Lincoln's only protection the night he died. "This time Pinkertons will be guarding the President."

"We will, but I'll be honest with you." In the pale sunshine leaking through the dusty window, Harry Barnett's eyes were tiny points of light. "Since you quit on us so suddenly, we ain't been able to replace you. We don't have as many experienced operatives on this job as we'd like. The old man is worried about anything that looks like a possible threat to President Arthur. You were always close to Allan. Don't let the old man down, now. Take Garrett and Rockefeller up on their offer. Spend a few days finding out who arranged the deaths of Rubman and his friends and why."

Oliver drained his mug. "You always did have a flim-flam tongue, Harry. It's not the old man who wants me in on this, it's you. You're the party responsible for guarding the bigwigs. If something happens, you're the one whose neck will be on the chopping block. Am I correct?"

Harry's cheeky grin acknowledged the truth.

Oliver chuckled. "You're a hard man to resist, but no sale. I said I was finished, and I meant it. I'm starting a new life for myself and my daughter, and I'll not go back on that to save your skin."

The smile left Harry's eyes. "Then sign on with Garrett and Rockefeller to save your own skin."

"What?"

"Maybe you're tired of blood now, Oliver, but you've got a bloody history. According to a little bird in Philly, there's a murderer on your trail, old friend."

"It wouldn't be the first time. I can take care of myself."

"What about your new daughter? A word from me will put him out of action. But you have to return the favor."

"Who is this killer?"

"I'll speak his name after you've given me your word that you'll do this railroad job. Oh, and there's one more thing. You told Rockefeller you weren't going to work for him because you intended going into business for yourself?"

Oliver nodded.

"He says if you don't find who's responsible for destroying that railroad car, he'll make sure that any business you go into fails. He can do it. You've seen him do it with your own eyes, am I right?"

CHAPTER FIVE

L ate that afternoon Oliver inspected the burned husks of the runaway coal car and the private car in which Enoch Rubman, Ben Magruder and Ira Nutwell had died.

The derailed remains of both had been moved off the main track. Only a few timbers of the original yellow wood private car were still intact. Under the blistering summer sun the charred wood and twisted metal were still hot to the touch.

Standing on the siding next to the switch with sweat pooling under his arms, he pictured the accident--felt the searing heat of the explosion, smelled the acrid smoke, heard the shrieks of terror. West of the track, a bird called mournfully. He opened his eyes in time to see it spread its wings and drift off over the treetops.

The train had been stopped to make way for a freight. The coal car had been parked on the siding. Presuming that the telescoping was not really an accident, someone could have been waiting to throw the switch and release the handbrake on the coal car. The one percent grade would have taken care of the rest. But all this depended on split second timing. Who would have had the knowledge and will to pull it off?

Too damn many candidates, Oliver thought. He scratched the back of his head. If the target wasn't Rockfeller or the railroad, somebody on the train might have seized a random opportunity to kill one of the men in that car. More than three hundred passengers had been riding the train that night.

On the other hand, Rubman had known for twenty-four hours that he would have the use of the car. He might have told someone else, someone who wanted him dead and knew how to throw a railroad switch.

Riding back to town, Oliver fumed. Harry had tricked him into taking on this quagmire of a case and cheerfully admitted that the killer he'd used as bait was a ruse.

"Olly old pal, such is my love for you that I put the miscreant out of commission before I left Philly. You've got nary a care."

"So it was an idle threat. Did this villain even exist?"

"He was real enough. You remember the Lewis gang? We put 'em in jail, but vigilantes strung 'em up before they got the minor courtesy of a trial."

"I haven't forgotten."

Like the Jameses and the Renos, the Lewises had been wild young men schooled in violence by the war. When the south surrendered, they hadn't cared to go back to a hardscrabble life on a Missouri farm. They'd turned to robbing banks for money and thrills.

"Johnny Lewis was only three when his older brothers swung. Now he's eighteen and pried from the same mold," Harry explained. "He was braggin' in a bar on how he planned to gun you down. My man overheard him and brought me the story. I took care of it."

"Took care of it how?"

"Let's just say that at the present moment little Johnny isn't in a condition to gun anybody down."

Oliver had been too angry to ask for details. "Damn your lies, Harry! There's no killer after me."

"Thanks to my strenuous efforts on your behalf. You should be on your knees expressing gratitude."

"You damned schemer! What's to keep me from turning my back on you!"

"Just your word, old friend, and the knowledge that you'll have John D. Rockefeller hounding you to the ends of the earth to make sure you're ruined."

It was late when Oliver got home from viewing the remains of the train wreck. As he shut the door behind him Mrs.

Milawney came out of the back hall wiping her hands on her apron. "Oh there you are, sir. There's a lady waiting in the front parlor, name of Mrs. Hannah Kinchman. Says she has important business with you."

"What sort of business?"

"She wouldn't say, sir, but she's old and talks real starchy-like. I thought maybe she might be a friend of your aunt's."

He was bone tired and hungry. "How long has Mrs. Kinchman been waiting?"

"Over an hour, sir. She came just after Chloe and me got back from our walk."

"How is Chloe?"

Mrs. Milawney smiled. "Upstairs playing with her dolls and quite contented. She does love those dollies of hers. A sweet child if ever I saw one, sir."

"Good. I'll have dinner with her after I see my visitor." He slid open the pocket doors to his left and walked into his aunt's small parlor.

A humpbacked old lady with iron gray hair and a face like a withered apple sat on the edge of a tufted chair. Her feet, encased in black kid, were firmly planted on the Turkey rug. She was conservatively dressed in a suit of golden brown poplin, her only jewelry a hair brooch framed in jet.

"Mr. Redcastle, I presume?" Her voice creaked like a rusty gate, but had that indefinable something that suggested money and class.

"How may I help you, Mrs. Kinchman is it?"

"Mrs. Hannah Kinchman. I've come to you on a matter of business. I'm in need of the services of a private detective. It's to do with a female servant in my household. I believe she's stealing my jewelry. I'd like proof. Can you help me?"

"Can I inquire where you got my name?"

"From the Pinkerton Agency. I wrote to them asking for a reference and they gave me you."

"I'm afraid they've misdirected you, Mrs. Kinchman. I'm no longer doing detective work, and even if I were, I'd be unable to help you. Domestic matters such as yours are outside my purview."

"But they wouldn't be if you had a woman working for you, now would they?"

He arched an eyebrow. "That's true enough, but I don't employ a female detective."

"But you easily could." Mrs. Kinchman's voice had changed in timbre from that of an old woman to that of a young one.

Oliver stared as his visitor continued to metamorphose. Her back straightened, her skin smoothed out. When she lifted her hand and removed a gray wig, the transformation was complete. She leapt up and handed him a letter. "If you would be so good as to read that, it will explain my reason for being here and the little trick I just played on you."

The letter was from Allan Pinkerton. "Ollie, my boy, this young lady ought to suit you to a T." In glowing terms, it recommended Mrs. Kinchman to Oliver as a possible operative in his new detection agency.

"Very clever," he said dryly. "You had me fooled completely."

"Thank you."

He studied her. She was medium height and slim. Though her features were regular and delicately formed, he would not have described her as pretty. She neither blushed nor flinched at his examination, but returned his scrutiny with level gray eyes.

He said, "Allan Pinkerton wrote this letter from his home in Chicago. Chicago is a long way for a young woman to travel on the off chance of employment."

"Actually, I received that letter from Mr. Pinkerton in the mail and took the train down from Philadelphia."

"You were working in the Philadelphia office?"

"For a time, but I was not well accepted there and asked Mr. Pinkerton to give me another recommendation."

Oliver nodded. Since hiring Kate Warne when he first started his agency, Allan Pinkerton had been a strong advocate of using females as operatives. Other men did not share his opinion. He had sent several women to the Philadelphia office, but they had regularly been rejected by his sons. Had Harry Barnett known that Mrs. Kinchman was planning to present herself in Baltimore in this outrageous fashion, Oliver wondered. Or were the two incidents unconnected?

He folded the letter and handed it back. "Impressed though I am with your talents at acting and disguise, I'm not planning to open my own detection agency, and I have no use for a female operative. I'm sorry you've made such a long trip for nothing."

"Then you're like the others, prejudiced against females?"

"Not at all. I knew and admired Kate Warne's work. I'm well aware that women can go certain places and learn certain things that men can't. You didn't need to trick me with that charade."

"I see. Rather than impressing you, I've angered you."

"That's not the case."

"Then why won't you give me a chance to show you what I can do?"

"What makes you think you'd make a good detective, Mrs. Kinchman?"

"Before applying to Mr. Pinkerton for a job, I was an actress in Texas. He seemed to think that was good background."

"You don't sound like a Texan."

"I can use several different accents." She ran through a repertory of accents from southern belle, to Irish washerwoman. In Oliver's ear, they all sounded plausible.

"All right, I'm dazzled. I still don't have a job for you. I'm sorry, but you've made the trip for nothing."

She shrugged. "Maybe not. Baltimore appears to be quite a thriving spot. I noticed several theaters doing good business. Now that I'm here, I might as well stay a few days." She handed him a card. "I've taken a room at Miss Battaile's Boarding House on Cathedral Street. If you should change your mind, you can look me up there."

Oliver accepted the card, but he knew he wasn't going to change his mind.

CHAPTER SIX

The next morning Garrett arranged for Oliver to speak with employees who'd been on the Capital Express the night of the accident.

Inside the B&O roundhouse the clang of arriving and departing trains rang off the walls as if Hephaestus, the blacksmith god of the ancient Greeks, were hammering at a giant anvil.

Amidst the din, Oliver interviewed a frightened looking youth named Cyrus Roe who'd served Rubman, Magruder and Nutwell their dinner on the fatal night.

"How did the three men strike you?"

Roe gazed up at Oliver anxiously. "Very jolly, sir. They were laughing almost the whole trip."

"What were they laughing about?"

"I don't remember, sir."

"I know it's your job to be invisible. But Rubman was an important man. It's only natural you would be curious about him and his friends. What kind of jokes were they telling?"

Roe's freckled neck reddened. "Oh, about the war, sir, and the, the usual."

"What's the usual?"

"About women."

"Anything in particular about women?"

"They left off talking when they noticed I'd come in, sir, so I didn't hear much. I think the other two men were teasing Mr. Rubman about being irresistible to women and that. Just men's talk, you know."

"I see." Oliver dismissed the young man and called in his next interview subject, the conductor.

"How would you describe Mr. Rubman?" Oliver asked the

middle-aged man.

"Very nice fella. Always had a smile and a hello, if you know what I mean. Terrible what happened."

"Do you have any notion how it could have happened?"

He tugged at the Van Dyke decorating his chin. "I've been thinking about that, and it's a puzzler. Can't see how it could have been deliberate. We weren't stopped for that freight more'n ten minutes."

"But it wouldn't have taken more than five minutes to throw the switch and release the handbrake. Someone who knew the freight was on the schedule might have done it."

"Who? Half the time we would have missed the freight, anyway. Lots of things can delay a train. It must have been an accident."

"Isn't it possible that somebody aboard the train who knew railroading and this line in particular might have seen an opportunity for murder and taken it?"

The conductor paled. "Nobody who works with me on that line would have done what you're saying. They're all good people."

"Did Mr. Rubman often use private cars?"

"No more than the other bosses. They all entertain their friends now and again. I tell you, maybe somebody wanted to kill those other two. Mr. Rubman, everybody liked him. What happened was an accident, pure and simple."

The morning wore on in that vein. After hearing a Greek chorus of praise for Rubman, Oliver decided to visit the man's widow.

First, however, he went home. He found Chloe playing in the small garden behind the house. He paused at the top of the porch, a tightness constricting his chest as he took in the idyllic scene. The hot June sun filtered through a canopy of new leaves, mottling the brick walkway and glinting on Chloe's tumbled red-gold curls. Absorbed in giving her dolls a tea party, she didn't notice him.

Six months earlier, he'd been holed up in a Chicago boarding house fighting his way through a bout of malaria. Unshaven, half delirious, he'd staggered out of the tangle of his sweat-drenched bedclothes to answer a rap on his door only to be struck dumb by the sight of a little girl.

A drab, older woman holding the girl's hand introduced herself as Mrs. Brill and said, "The child's name is Chloe. Her mother, Marietta Dumont, is dead. Her gentleman friend left and she stopped paying me, but I stayed to nurse her. Now that she's gone, I can't keep her child. I found out your address from the Pinkertons. I hope you're her father, like Miss Dumont said, because I used the last of her money on train fare. Either you take the little thing or she goes to an orphanage. Which is it to be?"

When Chloe had realized that she was to be left with this gaunt, unshaven man, she had fallen onto the floor in hysterics. Though he had tried to comfort her, she had rejected him utterly and still did. She no longer wept at the sight of him, but she remained uncommunicative, gazing at him like a little sphinx and answering his questions in nervous monosyllables.

He couldn't imagine what was going through her mind. How had she been affected by her mother's death? How did she feel about being thrust upon a man who was a total stranger to her? What did she make of being told the man was her papa and she must love and obey him?

Chloe looked up from her play. The animation drained from her face and her eyes grew wary.

"I thought I'd join you for lunch," Oliver said. He walked down the steps and crossed through a patch of shadow. "That's a fine looking party you're having."

For the first time, he noticed who was at the party and who wasn't. When Mrs. Brill had turned Chloe over to him, the child had possessed three small dolls, all of them dingy from use. Black hair had been crudely painted onto their cheap china heads. Trying to win his newfound daughter's affection, he had spent more money than he could afford on a large doll with a golden mane of human-hair curls flowing from its fine bisque china head. Never having bought a gift for a little girl before, he felt awkward and uncertain.

"This is Miss Pringle," Oliver had joked when he'd presented Chloe with the gift. Chloe's jaw had dropped and her eyes had widened. He'd thought she was pleased. But now, he observed with a sinking heart, Miss Pringle was nowhere in sight.

"Miss Pringle is sick," Chloe said, apparently guessing what was in his mind. "She doesn't feel well enough to go to parties."

"I'm sorry to hear that. Perhaps she'll feel better later on. Do you think she might?"

"I don't know," Chloe answered, looking everywhere but at him.

He kept the disappointment out of his voice. Would he ever win her over, this child who might or might not be his? "Come," he said, taking her hand despite her obvious reluctance, "Mrs. Milawney has fixed us a delicious lunch of cold chicken and salad. There's fresh squeezed lemonade, too."

Felicia Rubman lived in a large house recently built north of the boundary on the county side of North Avenue. After Oliver paid off his hack, a thin man dressed in a black frock coat and string tie came hurrying out the front door. Distractedly, he nodded and then climbed into his jagger. Since he carried a medical bag, Oliver presumed he must be a doctor. Curious, he watched him drive off.

A few minutes later a round-faced Irish maid garbed in black to signify that the household was in mourning, led Oliver to the drawing room where the windows were draped in black crepe to shut out the light.

In the gloom he waited amidst tufted chairs and settees and a forest of glass-topped table cabinets stuffed with innumerable tiny china dogs, cats, and elephants. On the wall overlooking them was a gilt mirror draped with black crepe. A black wreath of silk and wax flowers hung on the mantel.

Felicia Rubman herself looked rather like a poodle. A tuft

of glossy mahogany curls perched atop her small, round head. Strands of curling hair hung in front of her ears. They framed a pale but still plump and pretty face dominated by doe-like brown eyes. Signifying her mourning, her black silk dress molded her full breasts tightly and failed to disguise that she was in a late stage of pregnancy.

As Oliver introduced himself, Mrs. Rubman gazed up at him with a lost expression. Touched by her feminine vulnerability, he offered condolences, explained his reason for being there, and questioned her gently.

"Mrs. Rubman, do you know of anyone who might have wished to harm your husband?"

Her pink mouth opened. "Harm Enoch? Why, why no, no I don't. But why do you ask? The crash was an accident, wasn't it?" Her voice quivered and then sank. She dabbed at her eyes with the damp lace handkerchief she clutched.

"That's what's generally believed, but we have to consider all the possibilities. Are you sure you know of no one who might have held a grudge against your husband? Very few men in positions of power are entirely without adversaries."

A faint blush came to Felicia Rubman's cheek. "Enoch never talked to me of such things. If he had enemies, he never spoke of them."

"Who were his friends and associates?"

"The men he worked with. The men at his club, I suppose. He liked gymnastics. He worked at swinging Indian clubs with a Professor Bombick at the YMCA."

"Professor Caleb Bombick? He still teaches physical culture at the Y?"

Mrs. Rubman nodded. "That's all I know, really. Now, please, please, I'm not well."

Oliver handed her a card. "I'm sorry to distress you. If you remember anything that you think might be important, or if you wish to speak to me about anything whatsoever, you'll find me at that address."

She accepted the card, then pressed her handkerchief to her

mouth. "It's all to much!"

As Oliver made apologetic noises, a golden-haired toddler stumbled into the room. "Mama, Mama!" Eluding the nursemaid who pursued him, the child launched himself at his mother.

With a sob, Felicia Rubman sank to her knees and caught the boy up in her arms. She mashed him to her bosom and began to weep into his curls. "Oh, poor, poor baby. Poor, poor fatherless baby!"

Oliver caught the look the maid bent on her mistress. It held sympathy, but also scorn. As she showed Oliver out, he turned on the threshold. "This is a sad time for your mistress."

"Oh, very sad, sir."

"I see that Mrs. Rubman is expecting another child. How many children are there in the house now?"

"Two, sir."

"On the way into the house, I met a doctor leaving. Was he attending Mrs. Rubman or her children?"

"Why, that would be Doctor LeSane. He's famous in these parts--attends all the fine ladies who are on the increase. Naturally, Mrs. Rubman has been feeling poorly."

"Of course."

"Lucky my lady is to have parents in Baltimore who'll look after her."

"That is a good thing. Did Mr. Rubman have family, here as well?"

"Not that I know of, sir. His people come from out west. He has a brother who lives off in Pensylvania."

"Indeed? Were he and his brother on good terms?"

"I wouldn't know, sir. I never seen the brother."

"Yet Mr. Rubman seems to have been quite the family man."

"Family man?" A look of bitter humor came into the girl's eyes.

An alarm went off in Oliver's head. "A home loving man. Would you describe your master as a home loving man?"

The girl's face closed. "I'm sure Mr. Rubman was a good husband and father, sir."

"What is your name?"

"Mary, my name is Mary McClarty. Now, I got to get back to my work." Firmly, she shut the door in his face.

Since Oliver had dismissed his hack, he decided to walk until he came across a livery. Tossing his jacket over his shoulder, he set off down the road and reviewed his impressions of the Rubman household.

How much did Felicia Rubman really know about her husband? Either she had been withholding information about Enoch's associates, or he'd kept her in the dark. Many men kept their domestic life separate from their business and other personal relationships. In such cases their wives were mewed up in their houses, their entire emotional beings focused on their children. Oliver could believe that Felicia Rubman was such a woman.

But not everyone in the Rubman house was so unobservant or ignorant. That sharp-eyed maid, Mary McClarty, for instance. She knew more than she was telling. But how to get the information out of her?

He was mulling over the possibilities when his knee twinged. As he leaned over to rub his old war wound a bullet whizzed past his ear and knocked his hat off. Instinctively, he fell forward and rolled off the side of the road. He kept rolling until he found cover behind a large pine tree.

He lay breathing hard. The fallen pine needles at the base of the tree pricked his neck and hands. He shifted position, expecting another shot. None came. At length he peered through the pine boughs. He could see a thick grove of similar trees on the far side of the road. That must be where his attacker had hidden, and was hiding still. The whicker of a horse confirmed this hypothesis. But who the hell was it? Oliver knew enough about guns to recognize the sound of a Navy Colt. And he was unarmed. He cursed himself for his stupidity.

Cautiously, he took his handkerchief out of his pocket, tied it to a stick and waved it where the gunman might think it part of his shirt. Nothing. Then he heard hooves. He inched to his feet. A cloud of dust hung over the trees from which the shot had been fired. A hundred yards to the east of them a horse and rider disappeared over the crest of a hill.

CHAPTER SEVEN

Two hours later a footsore Oliver climbed to the second floor of the Young Men's Christian Association. At the top he ran into a wall of noise accompanied by cigar smoke and whiskey fumes commingled with the pungent tang of un-bathed male bodies. A knot of men cheered and hooted around the boxing ring set up in the center of the gymnasium. One of the men sparring in tights was John L. Sullivan, the American boxing champion.

Fascinated, Oliver watched as Sullivan's scrappy opponent gave as good as he got. Though Sullivan knocked him to the canvas several times, he bounced right up and came back punching. A referee called time and the two men shook hands. Surrounded by several jovial, cigar-puffing and tobacco chewing companions, Sullivan disappeared into the wash room.

"Good God! As I live and breathe, it's Oliver Redcastle all grown up!" Caleb Bombick, professor of physical culture at the YMCA, wove the thick shuttle of his robust, short-legged body past a network of hanging rings, canvas mats and wood and leather pommel horses.

As Oliver stuck out his hand, twenty years seemed to drop away. "Professor, you haven't changed."

Less hair adorned Bombick's bullet head, and the full beard nesting about his thick neck was grizzled. Otherwise, the instructor looked as formidable in his black tights and sash as he had when Oliver had been a boy of fourteen.

"Was that fellow in the ring just now who I think it was?"

"John L. Sullivan himself," the professor acknowledged with a twinkle. "He's come down from New York for the encampment. You could have knocked me over with a feather when he strolled in. I thought my man gave him a mighty fine workout."

Oliver eyed the other fighter's carroty curls and bulldog build. Instead of going to the showers like Sullivan, he was dancing around a punching bag.

"I'm impressed," Oliver allowed.

"And so you should be. His name's Danny Coy. I pay him to spar with my clients." Bombick looked Oliver over. "I'm impressed, myself. Ollie, I believe you're more changed than Griff."

At the mention of his cousin's name, Oliver's smile stiffened. They'd met during the summers he'd spend in Baltimore with his Aunt Vera. It had been Griff who'd introduced him to Professor Bombick's physical culture studio. After their lessons with the professor, the boys had cemented their friendship by spending happy hours exploring Baltimore's waterfront.

Oliver still remembered the creak of hawsers against thick wood pilings as the eastern shore's bugeyes, skipjacks and Baltimore clippers rocked with the tide on those hot summer afternoons.

He asked, "How is Griff?"

"Married that pretty girl, Laura Wilburn. You remember her, don't you?"

"How could I forget?"

"Seems to me you were sweet on her yourself."

"I was. Does Griff still come here?"

"Rarely. His problem makes vigorous exercise difficult."

"Problem?"

"Didn't you know? The poor boy lost his sight in the war."

Oliver hadn't known. Though he'd maintained an irregular correspondence with his aunt, she'd never mentioned Griff's disability. "I'm sorry to hear of it."

"You could tell the fellow that yourself. I suppose you must know that when your flint-hearted old bastard of a grandfather died, Griff inherited the Singleton property. He lives there now."

The Professor slapped Oliver's shoulder. "All right, Griff fought sesesh and you fought union. But that was near twenty years ago. Time you young bucks admitted the war's water under the bridge. Enough said. What about yourself? You look fit enough. Eating right?"

Recalling that the professor subscribed to Sylvester Graham's regimen of taking cold-water baths with regular exercise and renouncing coffee, tea, whiskey, tobacco and large servings of meat, Oliver shook his head. "Until recently, I was a traveling man. Couldn't always be choosy about eats."

The professor harumphed. "Can't have harmed you. Your belly's flat as a top hat under a wagon wheel." His fist snapped out and Oliver leapt back just in time to avoid a sharp blow to his midsection. Bombick chortled. "I see that limp doesn't slow you down when you need to use your feet. War wound?"

"Minie ball."

"Lot of men walking around with those. Keeping your fists in trim, are you?"

"I search out a match when I get the chance."

Sullivan emerged from the dressing rooms wearing a bowler and check suit. His voice boomed over the heads of his throng of admirers. "I've had me daily constitutional, so I'm ready to eat the city bare!"

As he passed by Danny Coy, he flipped him a silver dollar, tipped his hat to the professor and sauntered out of the gym with his cronies.

When he was gone, the professor steered Oliver across the gym. "There's someone here you should meet." He pointed at a thick-waisted man with a blond walrus moustache huffing and puffing in the corner with a pair of dented Indian clubs. "What do you think of that fellow?"

"I'd say he's badly outmatched by those clubs."

Bombick laughed. "You'd be right. Bailey's banker's bum is far too fond of padded chairs. Here, I'll introduce you." He called out, "Say, Edson, you might be wanting to meet this fella. From what I hear, he saved your little girl from a bad setup the other day."

Oliver connected the name Bailey with the child Annie Bailey he'd rescued from Flatt. This must be her banker father.

Bailey dropped his clubs. His broad pink face lit with a mixture of surprise and that instinctive distaste a man with power feels at the prospect of being indebted to another he conceives to be of lesser importance. He stuck his hand out and Oliver briefly took it.

"I've been meaning to come see you so I could express my appreciation properly," Bailey said.

"No need for that. How's your daughter?"

"Fine. A bit shaken still, but well enough. I was out of town when the incident occurred. So was Marshal Rackley's sharpshooter, Gloger. That man's a wonder with a gun, but you must be close to his equal. Maybe the two of you should meet." Bailey wiped his sweating neck. "I've an appointment in half an hour's time, so I can't linger. Stop by my bank when you have an opportunity, Redcastle. It's the Monument National. I'll have a reward for you."

While Bailey hurried off to change clothes, Bombick turned to Coy who was hammering at a sawdust bag as if he meant to disembowel it with his fists.

"Can it be that John L. Sullivan himself hasn't pounded the stuffings out of you?"

"Are you daft," Coy shot back scornfully. "Going three rounds with that overrated Mick was like sitting in me easy chair reading me Sunday paper."

"That being the case, do you think you could give this gent here a round or two?"

Coy looked Oliver up and down, then smirked. "I believe I'm up to it."

"Not today," Oliver said. "Somebody just took a pot shot at me while I was walking into town."

"You don't say?" For the first time Bombick seemed to notice the dirt stains on Oliver's trousers.

After dismissing Coy, who backed off sulkily, Bombick picked a pine needle out of Oliver's sleeve and led him to the washroom.

Standing back to watch as he cleaned up, he asked, "Now,

why would anybody take a shot at you and then ride off like that."

Oliver rolled up his sleeves and poured a pitcher of water into a bowl. "I'd like the answer myself."

"Your Aunt Vera told me you'd turned into a Pinkerton."

"A Pinkerton detective is on the side of law and order. What I did all those years was legal."

"Maybe, but some say it's just murder hiding behind a badge. After what Quantrill did to your folks, Vera worried about you turning bitter enough to take pleasure in hunting men for revenge. And revenge, as we all know, corrupts the soul."

Oliver stared at his grim image in the shaving mirror. "When did she say all this to you, Professor?"

"Just before she died. I believe her worries for your everlasting soul were part of what prompted her to leave you her house and fortune. That and the fact your grandfather left you nothing. I hope you don't resent Griff Singleton because he received all of your mother's family fortune."

"I'm doing my damndest not to, Professor. I've come to Baltimore to change my life."

"That's happy news. Why did you come here after getting shot and not to a police station?"

"The police aren't going to help when I can't even describe my attacker. I only saw the back of him. He wore a long coat and had his head covered with a hat." Oliver mopped his face with a wet towel. "Do you know a railroad man named Enoch Rubman?"

"The one killed in that accident last week? I should smile. He used to come here regular. Why?"

"I've taken a job with the B&O investigating his death."

"I thought you said you were planning to change your life?"

"This investigation is my last case. I'm not even carrying a weapon. Hadn't thought I'd need one. Out on the road, with bullets whizzing around my ears, I reconsidered."

The professor nodded. "Baltimore's got its share of blood and guts. Things will get worse when the encampment works up a head of steam. I know a good man for weapons. Barroso's pawn shop is on Fayette."

"Thanks for the tip. Now, what can you tell me about Rubman?"

"Handsome devil. Quite the ladies man. Do you think whoever shot at you was connected with Rubman?"

"I've no notion, but it's an idea. Who would want to see him dead?"

"You're talking murder, not accident?" Bombick whistled. "Most people, including me, liked Enoch Rubman. However, if pressed, I guess there might be more than one jealous husband who didn't hold the man in high esteem."

This jibed with what the waiter on the train had said, and fit the knowing expression in the Rubman maid's eyes. Oliver secured his celuloid collar and snapped his suspenders over his shoulders. "Can you name names?"

"Sorry. I'm an abstemious man myself and when it comes to my clients' private lives, I close my ears to gossip. If there's information of that sort to be had, you'll have to find it elsewhere. Rubman was a regular customer at Mrs. Kitty Putnam's establishment in Fells Point."

"And what is that?" Oliver asked, though he'd guessed.

"The best whore house in Baltimore."

CHAPTER EIGHT

Mrs. Kitty Putnam's door was opened by one of the prettiest girls Oliver had ever seen. She had huge pansy-colored eyes, pearly skin and hair the color and texture of black silk. She also had an Irish brogue so thick he could barely understand her. Dressed in plain servant's garb, she conducted him to Mrs. Putnam's office.

There, Oliver listened as that lady declared, "Enoch Rubman hasn't been around here in three months."

"Why is that, do you suppose?"

Mrs. Putnam's sharp face closed. She was a thin little woman who parted her graying hair down the center and pulled it back in a severe bun. Dressed entirely in black, she looked more like a school marm than the owner of a fancy house catering to Baltimore's growing population of lawyers and businessmen.

"Discretion is my stock and trade right along with a bit of healthy fun. I don't discuss clients," she informed Oliver, "former or otherwise. I'm sorry to hear of Mr. Rubman's accident, but there's nothing I can tell you about him. Now, if you'll excuse me, I have a busy afternoon."

Briskly, she ushered Oliver into her front hall. Unlike her austere office, it was papered in red and decorated with gilt mirrors and French-style furniture. A thin man dressed in a black frock coat and string tie came hurrying down the stairs. Above the soft plop of his footfalls on the thickly carpeted steps, Oliver heard female voices on the upper floor. He pictured women lounging in filmy lingerie with their hair unbound and their flesh moist from sleep and sex. This pleasant image receded as he recognized the man. It was the same physician he'd seen coming out of Felicia Rubman's house carrying what looked like the same medical bag.

"I've examined them all," he told Mrs. Putnam. "Jenny's got a cold for which I've prescribed tincture of lobelia mixed with bloodroot and oil of spearmint. For Sadie's chronic problem with mucous surfaces I've written out a fine recipe for hard balsom copaiba, fresh ground cubebs and carbonate of ammonia. One pill three times a day between meals. Otherwise, all clear."

Mrs. Putnam extracted a huge roll of bills from the cloth purse she kept on her belt. After she had peeled several off the top, the doctor snatched them, tipped his hat and hurried out the front door.

Oliver asked, "Does Doctor LeSane come here often."

Mrs. Putnam gave him another of her pinched looks. "Not as a customer, if that's what you're thinking. The man's far too busy running here and there seeing to every woman in this city. I have him check my girls for the pox once a month. That's more than any other establishment in Baltimore. I run a clean house."

A few hours later this statement was confirmed by Antonio Barroso, proprietor of Barroso's pawn shop. "A man who wants a high class roll in the hay can't do better than Kitty Putnam. You'd never guess now, but she used to be the toast of New Orleans."

Oliver had stopped into Barroso's fascinating emporium on his way home. He inspected the weaponry jamming the Italian pawnbroker's shelves, counters and glass cases. The pleasant aroma of cold steel and oiled wood mixed with dust, metal filings and sheep tallow lubricant filled the shop.

"I see you looking at the Lancaster." The thin ends of Barroso's waxed moustache quivered as he pointed at a display of muzzle-loaders on the wall behind him.

"I was admiring the McCoy squirrel rifle under it."

Barroso took the rifle down and handed it over. The oiled stock slid under Oliver's arm like silk, stirring memories. "That was my first rifle, the McCoy. A drifter gave it to me just before he died. I helped him into town after he got bit by a rattlesnake. By then he knew he wasn't going to survive. I was ten years old."

"I'll wager you were one happy young'un to get that gun."

Oliver nodded. He'd been thrilled all right. But he'd figured his father wouldn't approve, so he'd kept it hidden. His father had discovered him with the McCoy, accused him of stealing the weapon and beaten him with a strap to get him to admit his transgression. His mother had stopped the beating by running into town and recruiting Mr. Reems at the General Store to back up his story about the drifter. In the end, due to his mother's intercession, Oliver had kept the McCoy. From that day he'd treasured it the way a pirate might his horde of gold.

"Do you still have that old rifle?" Barroso took the fine old weapon from his hands and replaced it.

"Lost it in the war. I still dream about it sometimes. Those were the days, when I was a boy hunting alone, just me, my dog and that gun. I've never been happier than I was then."

A half hour later he left Barroso's shop wearing a Remington double barreled over-under derringer strapped to his right calf. In his hand he carried a silver-headed cane capable of discharging a .41 caliber bullet.

Harry Barnett claimed Johnny Lewis had been neutralized. Maybe so, Oliver thought as he wove through the obstacle course of horse cars, wagons and carriages that littered the intersection of Baltimore and Calvert Streets. But somebody out there had tried to kill him this morning. If not Johnny, who?

Oliver walked into the Western Union office and sent a telegram to Allan Pinkerton. "Anybody looking for me?" Allan would know what that meant and put the word out on the grapevine. Oliver sent two other telegrams. One went to Benjamen Magruder's wife in Washington D.C., the other to Ira Nutwell's family in New Hampshire.

Outside again, Oliver glanced at the tangle of telegraph wires overhead and pondered Enoch Rubman's personal life. How complicated was it? In addition to keeping his young wife perpetually pregnant, he'd visited prostitutes. Had he maintained a mistress as well? Several mistresses? Might he have been killed by a jealous husband or lover? Why had he ceased visiting Kitty Putnam's establishment three months before his death?

A woman emerged from Brown's Bank building opposite. Oliver eluded a hack and caught up with her in front of a barber shop.

"Mrs. Kinchman?"

She stood in profile, gazing thoughtfully down at a window display of fat leeches advertising the barber's cupping and leeching services. When she heard Oliver's voice she turned her head. "Mr. Redcastle."

"I'm sorry if I startled you."

"I wasn't expecting to see you."

"Are you unwell? Do you have need of a leech?" He pointed at the bowl of pulsing worms.

"No!" She shuddered. "Surely you didn't stop me on the street to inquire after my health."

"Mrs. Kinchman, I hope I didn't seem unfriendly at our meeting the other afternoon. I'd had a long day and, quite frankly, I could see no reason why I might wish to make use of the services you offered."

"And now? Has that changed?"

The gray walking suit she wore bleached her features so that they seemed lost in general colorlessness, as if her face were an empty space on an otherwise pale canvas. Yet, as Oliver looked down at her, he noted that her bone structure was fine.

He said, "My needs may have changed. Are you still staying at Mrs. Battaile's Boarding House?"

"I am."

"How are you enjoying your visit in Baltimore? The city has quite a different flavor from Philadelphia's, wouldn't you agree?"

"Mr. Redcastle, what is it you wish to speak to me about?"

He pointed at the sign above a restaurant a few doors down. "It's a hot afternoon. May I offer you some refreshment?"

She hesitated, then nodded. "A glass of peppermint water would be pleasant."

When they were seated at a table in a window alcove, Mrs. Kinchman removed her gloves and untied her straw hat trimmed with oak leaves. A few strands of her fair hair came loose and caught the light from the window. For a split second, he wondered if she might have made herself look plain deliberately. Why would a woman choose to do that?

"Why are you looking at me so oddly?"

"I was trying to picture you on the stage. What sort of parts did you play?"

"All sorts. I was always a supporting actress, never the ingenue star. Sometimes I played comic roles, sometimes failing elderly aunts and mad spinsters. But versatility, I'm told, is a plus in detective work."

"It is. Where is Mr. Kinchman?"

"You don't shy at asking personal questions, do you?"

"Before I can offer you employment, there are certain things I need to know. Are you a widow?"

"Mr. Kinchman and I are separated. We do not live together and he does not contribute to my support."

"I see." Was there any Mr. Kinchman at all, Oliver wondered. She wore no wedding ring. Indeed, except for the hair brooch he'd noticed before, she wore no jewelry at all. Whose hairs were twined in that brooch, he wondered.

After the waiter brought their drinks and a plate of tea cakes, Oliver explained what he wanted.

Mrs. Kinchman sipped her beverage thoughtfully. "You wish me to discover what I can about this man Rubman's private life."

"Will you do it?"

"Yes."

"Good. The job is yours."

"I am to start by gaining the confidence of an Irish maid named Mary McClarty?"

"Do you think that's possible?"

"Faith and I don't see whyever not."

Her abruptly acquired Irish brogue startled Oliver. And it wasn't just the brogue. All at once her face looked different--

plumper, sturdier. But why should he be surprised? She was an actress and actresses were chameleons. He'd sat in theaters watching Chloe's mother charm the audience with her innocence when only a few hours earlier she'd played the wanton in his arms.

"Do you know an actress named Marietta Dumont?" he asked on impulse.

"I know of her. She was very beautiful, but she died recently if I'm not mistaken."

"She was the mother of my daughter."

Mrs. Kinchman looked startled. "I didn't know you had a daughter."

"Until recently, I didn't know myself." Oliver felt himself flush slightly. He'd just revealed a great deal more about his personal life than he'd intended. "Chloe lives with me now."

"Really? You accepted custody of this child when Marietta died? That was good of you. Is your daughter adjusting well to her new circumstances?"

"Not as well as I wish. She's a shy little thing. I frighten her."

"Why is that?"

"She misses her mother. It's hard for a child that young to lose a mother, and I suppose it was a shock to be plunged so abruptly into a life completely different from the one she'd known."

"Yes, it must. Though a child brought up in the theater would have to learn to be adaptable. How hard have you tried making friends with her? I've observed that most little girls adore their fathers if they're given half a chance."

"I confess I don't know much about children. I've bought new toys for her and instructed my housekeeper to buy her a new wardrobe. I gave her a beautiful doll named Mrs. Pringle which she never touches. She looks terrified whenever I walk into a room. When I speak to her, she hardly says more than yes or no."

Putting it into words forced Oliver to realize how much all this pained him. For all practical purposes, Chloe was the only family he had or was ever likely to have. Only now was he beginning to appreciate what a hollow and solitary life he'd led before Chloe had arrived at his door.

"Perhaps you're not spending enough time with your daughter. Why don't you take her to the theater?"

"She's young for a play, only seven."

"I saw my first theatrical performance at about that age, and I loved it. After all, your daughter's mother was an actress."

Oliver signaled for the check. "Perhaps I'll give your suggestion a try. In the meantime, do you need any further instructions?"

Mrs. Kinchman smiled cooly. "I think not. Be assured that when I have the information you wish, I'll call on you."

CHAPTER NINE

Bands of tri-colored bunting cascaded from the windows of the Eutaw House, headquarters of the commander-in-chief of the Grand Army of the Republic. As Oliver walked through the front door, a half dozen men dressed in Union blue hurried past loaded down with armfuls of paper scrolls.

Wading through the confusion, he got the attention of a volunteer clerk named Sanders. He was in his middle years, with a fringe of graying hair and a bristling Guard's moustache.

"I'm looking for information on three men, name of Enoch Rubman, Ira Nutwell and Ben Magruder."

After Oliver explained the circumstances, Sanders shook his head. "I served on the Summer Opera committee with Enoch. Fine fella. I'd like to help you, but we're run ragged here. Veterans are flocking in all wanting to link up with old chums. We're expecting twelve thousand veterans on parade day. It's pandemonium."

"The B&O brass is anxious to close this investigation. Think how many of your veterans are coming into the city in railroad cars."

Sanders looked surprised. "You're suggesting Enoch's accident wasn't really an accident?"

"No way of telling at this point."

"Give me your other victims' regiments. Perhaps I can find out something for you. Check with me tomorrow."

Oliver supplied what information he had gleaned from his visits to the Nutwell and Magruder families earlier that week, which was not a great deal. Magruder and his wife had been estranged for two years. According to his employer at a dry-goods store, he traveled to Baltimore on business frequently. His last recorded trip had taken place approximately two months before the accident.

Nutwell, a bachelor who ran a tobacco shop, had been a loner. Until the accident, he hadn't stirred from his hometown for years. Oliver had returned home feeling certain that the murderer, if he existed, was either local or connected in some way with the war and the present encampment. Either that or Rockefeller had been the target and Magruder, Nutwell and Rubman had been unlucky.

When Oliver left Eutaw House a miasma of pungent dust rose up from the cobbled street and hung in the air so thickly that it made his eyes water. After stopping at a Shaker stand to quench his thirst with a fresh-squeezed lemonade, he caught sight of a plainly dressed young woman showing her canvas gaiters as she lifted her skirts to climb onto a stepping stone laid across the gutter.

She paused in front of a shop window and he recognized her. It was the beautiful young Irish girl he'd seen at Kitty Putnam's. She hadn't looked like a prostitute then and she certainly didn't now. Attracted and curious, he was tempted to speak to her, but thought better of it.

In the street broughams, bicycles and mule cars vied for the right of way. On the corner a hot waffle man hawked his wares.

Turning off the busy thoroughfare, Oliver reached the sanctuary of his townhouse. While he'd been away looking up the Magruder and Nutwell families, he'd worried about Chloe's health and laid plans for improving their relationship. He was determined to win her over.

Mrs. Milawney had drawn the curtains against the heat and draped the pictures on the walls with cheesecloth. "To protect against bugs," she explained, taking his hat. "It's the fatal diseases they bring in with their dirty feet that kill us. Did you have a good trip, sir?"

"Middling. Where's Chloe?"

"I've got her in the tub, having her bath. Maybe cleanliness isn't a substitute for godliness, but it's mighty close."

"When she comes out, tell her I have a surprise. Tickets for "The Lady of the Camelias," with Sarah Bernhardt."

That night after supper Oliver was in his small library writing up a report on his interviews with the Magruders and Mrs. Nutwell when Mrs. Milawney tapped.

"There's a young man to see you, sir. Says he's with the railroad and you've talked to him before."

Cyrus Roe entered the room carrying his straw hat and looking nervous. "I hope I'm not disturbing you, sir."

"Not at all. Please take a seat."

He was trying to grow a moustache without much success. Above his cheap seersucker box coat his celluloid collar looked too tight.

"Have you remembered something new about the accident?"

"Nothing like that, sir, at least not exactly." Roe shifted his straw hat to his other hand, then shifted it back. "I thought I ought to speak to you about a thing I heard. This afternoon half our passengers were veterans come up from D.C. for the encampment."

"They're getting an early start."

"From what I hear, a lot of them have relatives in Baltimore or plan to stay with old friends. Anyhow, while I was serving the late lunch I overheard talk about one of the men killed in the accident, the man named Nutwell."

"Were the other two men mentioned?"

Roe shook his head. "A man said he was glad Nutwell was dead and that Nutwell deserved to burn in hell."

"Did he say why?"

That's all I heard, sir. I was very busy in the dining car. But the man who made that remark talked very fancy. His vest and cravat were both silk. He was clean-shaven and taller even than you. Maybe six-foot-four."

"You noticed this when he was sitting at a table?"

"I noticed it when he first walked into the dining car, before he'd said anything. There's something else. He wore a big watch, a silver model with a hunting case."

"Must be hundreds of those about."

"Not with a diamond mounted in the case, a real eye-blinder the size of a plover's egg. It had a gold plated minie ball dangling from the fob. I never saw a watch case and fob ornament like those before."

But Oliver had. Only one man that he knew fit the description Roe had just offered. His name was Gentleman Jake Jaggard. He was a thief with an international reputation, though no lawman had yet succeeded in pinning him with a crime. If Roe had truly seen Gentleman Jake, what was he doing in Baltimore? And what was his connection with Nutwell?

Before Roe disappeared into the night he left his address, and a promise to report back if he overheard more of interest. "I've dreamed of being a detective, sir. I know I could do the work. Maybe if I help you with this case, you'll think of me for others."

Reflecting on Roe's request, Oliver grimaced. He'd come to Baltimore to get away from detective work, yet already people were breaking down his door to be hired as sleuths. Feeling the beginnings of a headache, he closed his eyes.

He'd dreamed of dead soldiers at Antietam last night. He'd seen himself, a green boy of sixteen, picking them off at Bloody Lane. "Look for the brass." Those had been his instructions. So he'd loaded and reloaded until the barrel of his Springfield burned his hands. The thick puffs of black gunpowder rising up from it searing his eyes and the insides of his nostrils as he doggedly picked off the officers with the brass buttons and shiny gold epaulets. This morning he'd awakened with their screams in his ears.

He went upstairs to check on Chloe. She was having another bad night. While he was still on the staircase, he heard her labored breathing and his heart sank. Beneath her mosquito canopy, she was bathed in sweat.

He walked to the window and looked out. The walled garden at the back of the house would be cool and pleasant by this time, he thought. The dewy air would be easier to breathe.

On impulse, he went back to Chloe's bed, pulled up the mosquito canopy and scooped the sweating child into his arms. As her face came close to his, her eyes flew open then rolled wildly. She began to scream.

With so little oxygen in her lungs, her cries were pitiful, the mewlings of a terrified kitten. Still, they were loud enough to bring Mrs. Milawney spouting out of her bedroom in her shift.

"Good lord in heaven, what is it!" she exclaimed.

"I just thought I'd carry her into the garden so she could breathe easier, but I've scared her." He had to speak above Chloe's hysterical screams.

"I should say you have!" Mrs. Milawney wrestled Chloe from his arms. "Poor mite won't sleep for hours now!"

"I'm sorry. I wanted to help."

"You can help by leaving us." The woman sank her bulk into a rocking chair and settled the whimpering child in her lap. "I'll stay with her until she quiets down. Now shhh, shhh. Don't you cry. Your good old Mrs. Milawney is with you now, dearie."

He slunk away to his room at the other end of the hall and poured himself a whisky. For a long time he sat gazing out the window into the empty garden. By the time he finished his whisky, the house was quiet.

CHAPTER TEN

Sanders pointed at folders stacked high on his desk in the Eutaw House. "Your men are on top. I can't let you touch their files, but I can give you the salient facts."

He ticked off names and dates. Enoch Rubman and Ben Magruder had both served a two-year stint with the 125th Pennsylvania. Magruder had then been switched to the Fourth New Hampshire for the third year of his enlistment. He'd spent that final year as an officer at Point Lookout, the notorious camp for Confederate prisoners. Nutwell, also a three-year volunteer, had been promoted to Corporal in his final year.

"Anything dishonorable in Nutwell's record?"

"Nothing of that nature."

Then why had the man who sounded like Gentleman Jake said that Nutwell deserved to burn in hell, Oliver wondered. Tonight, after Chloe's play, he'd have a look at those forbidden files on Sanders' desk.

"Do you like the play?"

Chloe nodded mutely. Her ruffled pantalets just poked over the edge of the theater seat, and she clutched one of her old dolls, a ragged object named Delia. Lately, while the beauteous Mrs. Pringle stayed out of sight in Chloe's closet, Delia had become her constant companion. "Reminds the poor little thing of her mother, I dare say," Mrs. Milawney had explained to Oliver, as if he needed that spelled out.

He cast another anxious glance at his daughter. She seemed entranced by Sarah Bernhardt's performance. He'd worried that Chloe might be too young for a theater. But as he surveyed the rows of seats in front of them, he saw several youngsters near her age.

His roving gaze stopped, arrested by the profile of someone he knew two rows down and on the left. It was the Rubman's maid, Mary, dressed for an outing in a check suit with a double-breasted jacket. Who was the female next to her, the one laughing and talking with such animation?

She turned her head and he realized he was gazing at Mrs. Hannah Kinchman. No wonder he hadn't recognized her. With her gaudy lavender outfit and her hair a frizzy pouf, she looked like a barmaid.

Fascinated by this new transformation, Oliver stared. Apparently sensing his scrutiny, she turned and met his eyes. After that, he forced himself to look elsewhere.

When the performance ended, he had to concentrate on steering Chloe through the crowd. Out in the lobby, he looked around for Mrs. Kinchman, but she had disappeared.

"Oliver? Oliver Redcastle, is that really you?" A beautiful blond in a pink dress stood gazing up at him.

"Laura!"

"It is you!" Her silvery laugh rang out. "After all these years! Let me look at you. My goodness, what a handsome creature you've turned into. Smart as paint in those evening clothes and so tall and dark and, oh my, look at that moustache." She stood on tiptoe and tweaked the hair on his upper lip. "If only I'd known you were going to grow into such a lovely big man, I should have treated you more nicely."

Bemused, he said, "You've hardly changed at all, Laura. You're even more beautiful."

Laura Wilburn's family had lived two doors down from his Aunt Vera. In her sprigged muslins and Roman sandals, Laura hadn't been at all like the Quaker girls Oliver had known back home in Lawrence. They'd worn homespun dresses and thick-soled shoes, when they weren't going barefoot. None had possessed hair the color of sunlight or bewitching emerald eyes.

He'd never expected her to return his adoration and, except for a brief kiss one memorable Sunday morning, she hadn't. Her real interest had been in Griff, two years Oliver's senior and heir to the Singleton fortune. After the war, Vera had written to tell him that the two were married. "They were made for each other," he'd written back. "I wish them every happiness."

Still, Laura's face had never entirely faded from his memory. With good reason, he acknowledged. Despite the passage of two decades, she was a stunning woman.

"And who is this delectible child," she inquired? She knelt and gazed into Chloe's face.

Oliver introduced his daughter, who clasped Delia to her breast as if the wretched doll were a lifeline.

"Why, of course. I should have known at once. She looks exactly like you. Where is your wife? I'm dying to meet her. You must bring her for afternoon tea."

"Chloe's mother has passed away."

"Oh dear! Then you must bring Chloe for tea." Laura rose, withdrew a card from a fringed purse and stuffed it into his hand. "Come tomorrow at four and make things up with Griff."

"Laura, I. . ."

"You must. I won't let you deny me. Ollie, you and Griff are family and the war has been over for ages. The two of you used to be the best of friends, and you can be again. Now, I insist."

"Are you sure Griff wants to see me?"

"He will when I get through talking to him. You remember how sensitive he always was. Well, he's even more so now. But I can still make him see reason."

"Laura. . ."

"Did you know that he was grievously injured? He lost a good bit of his sight at Point Lookout."

"Point Lookout, the prison camp?"

"Yes, dreadful, dreadful! Now promise me you'll come. Promise!"

CHAPTER ELEVEN

"She fell asleep in the hack." Oliver carried Chloe over the threshold and into Mrs. Milawney's waiting arms.

The housekeeper looked sturdy and grandmotherly bundled up in a nightcap and cotton wrapper. "Let's hope the asthma don't have at her so bad tonight, sir. The trouble with sleep is the going to and the coming from, but it looks as if she's found her way." Her soft cheeks sagged into a network of tiny wrinkles as she gazed fondly at Chloe's sleeping face. "Did the little darling like the show?"

"Seemed to."

"It's good you took her, sir. She just needs to get to know you better. You can always get someone to love you. But it's like watching over a flower, don't you know? It opens when there's no one coaxing it but the sun."

Oliver watched as the woman carried Chloe upstairs. He was already laying plans for another outing. Perhaps they could spend a Sunday afternoon together in Druid Hill Park. They could rent a phaeton and take a spin around the Lake Drive. Chloe might enjoy seeing the thoroughbreds trotting with their silver bits and all the bustled belles lolling in cushioned broughams and Victorias.

Thinking of his disturbing chance meeting with Laura, he went to his room and took a hand-rolled cigar out of the box he reserved for special occasions. He'd smoke it in the garden.

Outside, while his eyes adjusted, he inhaled the fragrance coming off the grass mixed with the scent of his Aunt Vera's many flowers. Her roses blanketed a trellis forming a gateway into what had been her tiny herb plot.

The perfume rising from them brought Laura back into his mind. In particular, he remembered a hot afternoon in August and a picnic he'd shared in this garden with Laura and Griff. The three of them had feasted on fried chicken and biscuits and argued about the war. Griff had announced that he planned to slip over to the Eastern Shore and join the Confederate cause.

"Why don't you come with me, Olly? You never want to fight for the Union. You know what they call Lincoln, don't you? 'Old Ape.' Everybody hates him, even the abolitionists. If he gets an army together, it'll just be a bunch of big city riff raff and Irish scum recruited straight off the boat. The south has an army of gentleman. Besides, think what adventures we'll have together."

Oliver had refused. Both his parents were fervent abolitionists, and he, too, believed slavery was wrong. Lincoln or no Lincoln, he could never fight with so-called "gentlemen" who wanted to preserve it. In fact, if he did what his parents wanted he could never fight at all. His father was dead set against violence, even in a just cause. In his last letter he'd ordered Oliver to come home and not to think of enlisting.

"Oh Griff," Laura had exclaimed, "you might be killed!" She had slipped her hand into Griff's and his long, fine-boned fingers had closed around it so tightly that his knuckles showed white.

Oliver remembered how the sun had lit both their fair heads. At that moment, he'd realized that Laura, for all she loved to tease and flirt with him, would never be his. Two days later he'd gone against his father's wishes and joined up to fight for the Union.

Now, he struck a Blue Hen match on the heel of his leather boot. In the flare of light igniting his cigar he caught a slight movement on the other side of the trellis.

"Who's there?" He reached for the derringer strapped to his calf.

"Thank goodness you've appeared. There were no lights showing when I came to your house, so I decided to wait out here until you came home. I thought you might step out for a breath of air."

"Mrs. Kinchman?"

"Please lower your voice. You don't want us to be overheard, do you?"

Oliver walked through the trellis and into the shadows. She was sitting in a corner of the bench in an even deeper pool of obscurity. He could not make out her face at all.

"I saw you in the audience tonight. You were with the Rubman's maid," he said.

"You were staring at me."

"I'm sorry if I disconcerted you. You looked so different. At first I didn't recognize you."

"You did not disconcert me. And of course I looked different. I was playing the part of an Irish shopgirl in order to gain Mary McClarty's confidence. That's what you wanted, wasn't it?"

A thread of moonlight picked out the loose bird's nest of Mrs Kinchman's hair.

"You appeared to be on good terms with Mary, so you must have played your part well. Did you learn anything?"

"I'm here to report."

Her garments rustled as she adjusted her position. "According to Mary, Enoch Rubman was not faithful to his wife. In fact, he dallied with everything female that came his way, including poor Mary herself."

This did not surprise Oliver. He listened silently.

"The most interesting tidbit I gleaned from Mary has to do with a woman named Flora Penrose, the wife of Beacher Penrose."

"That name is familiar."

"He's a rather famous sculptor and portrait painter. He teaches at the Rinehart School of Advanced Sculpture at the Maryland Institute."

"What's the connection between Penrose's wife and Enoch Rubman?"

"According to Mary, Flora and Rubman were having an affair.

Three months ago she hung herself."

Three months. That was how long it had been since Enoch Rubman visited Kitty Putnam's establishment. Oliver crushed his cigar with the heel of his boot. "You seem to have a talent for winkling information out of Irish maids."

"I'll take that as a compliment."

"Would you like to try your hand at bigger game?"

"So long as you pay me, I'll try my hand at most anything."

He doled out the payment they'd agreed upon, and Mrs. Kinchman tucked the bills into the small string handbag she carried on her wrist.

He said, "I'd like to know more about Beacher Penrose. Specifically, I'd like to know if he was aware of his wife's affair. I'd also be interested to learn more details about her death. Do you think you can be of help?"

"I can certainly try." She rose. "I'll be in touch when I have what you want."

"How will you get back to your boarding house?"

"It's only a few blocks to Miss Battaile's. I'll walk."

"At this hour, I can't let you go alone. I'll see you home."

She didn't try to argue him out of it. After he let them out of the gate, they ambled along the quiet street in silence. A colored man stood outside the Mount Vernon hotel cleaning the street.

A Jagger raced past and Oliver recognized Doctor LeSane, doubtless hurrying to deliver a baby. Oliver wondered if any of his elegant patrons in the expensive Mount Vernon district knew that he also ministered to whores in Fells Point.

He glanced at the woman moving sedately next to him. What did he really know about her? "Tell me about yourself, Mrs. Kinchman."

"Why should I?"

"Why shouldn't you tell me your history? Why did you become an actress?"

"I was orphaned young and thrown onto the street with no education and a young brother to support. The only friend I could turn to was another actress I'd met."

"How did you meet her?"

"Family connections." Her tone was dry.

"So, she helped you take up the life."

"Yes."

"Acting is a romantic profession, yet you appear eager to leave it."

She laughed cynically. "Perhaps I was romantic as a young girl, Mr. Redcastle. I've had my illusions squeezed out of me." She pointed at a sturdy brick house across the street from the cathedral. "That's Miss Battaile's. You'll be seeing me again when I have information for you."

Oliver walked away thinking that now he had even more questions about Mrs. Kinchman. He turned the corner onto Monument where the lights were spaced more widely. After passing a bank, he paused in front of a shop window filled with an attractive arrangement of bottles of imported wine.

Though his aunt had left him a pleasantly furnished house and well cared for garden, the wine cellar was sadly lacking. When he had the opportunity, he planned to restock it. In fact, he hoped to restock every corner of his empty life. Somehow, he'd capture his daughter's trust. And when he was through untangling this mare's nest of a case, he'd invest in a respectable business. He'd put the past where it belonged, behind him.

He walked through a pool of shadow. A rough arm seized him by the throat and hauled him into the alley behind the bank.

CHAPTER TWELVE

Jabbing his elbow into his assailant's belly, Oliver turned sharply and pushed free of the attacker's grasp. "Coy!"

"The same, pantywaist. Time you learned to stop pokin' your nose where it don't belong. Say yer prayers!" Coy slammed his fist into Oliver's midriff.

He fell to the cobbles on his good knee. Coy had dragged him well into the alley. A sluggish surface drain coursed down its middle. Rats scrabbled amidst piles of trash. As he pushed himself to his feet, he spotted beady eyes peering at him from the shelter of a discarded corset.

"What the hell are you talking about, Coy?"

"I'll see the likes of you flat on your skinny arss in the stinkin' garbage!"

With his cap pulled low on his forehead, Coy jigged like a gorilla on a spring. His left fist jabbed out and Oliver dodged back. Coy waded in, but Oliver fought back with a solid right to his midsection. The young Irishman's belly felt like an oak log. The hit only deflected him for an instant.

Screaming gutter insults, he lowered his head and rushed. "Ringtail scum sucker! Mammy rammer!"

Stepping to his left, Oliver made a hammer of his fists and brought them both down on Coy's thick neck. As he shuddered under the blow, Oliver snapped his right knee into Coy's chin, then shoved his sagging body at a wood fence. The Irishman's head shattered a nine-inch wide board into pieces. Righting himself, he staggered around to face Oliver. The moonlight picked out streaks of blood oozing from puncture wounds. He pulled a six-inch splinter from his cheek and tossed it onto the cobbles.

"You bleedin' piece of shit. Stay out of my part of town!" He seized a three-foot length of the broken board and swung it at Oliver's head.

The edge caught his jaw and sent him staggering across the alley. He slammed into a board fence on the other side as Coy gathered himself for a rush. Shouts from the other end of the alley froze his assault. "Jaysus!"

Oliver wiped blood from his eyes. Three hulking shapes swarmed out of the shadows waving clubs and broken bottles. He reached for the derringer under his pantleg, but they ran past him and bore down on the retreating Coy.

"Beat the livin' shit out of the worm," the hooligan in front yelped as he jabbed a broken bottle at Coy's face.

The young Irishman swung his makeshift club. "Come near me, McKelvy, and I'll knock out your brains!"

Like hyenas closing in on a wounded animal, the other two thugs surrounded Coy. They seized his arms. Though he struggled savagely, they gradually pressed him up against the brick wall of a shed. McKelvey, their leader, chortled and swung his broken bottle back and forth.

"When I get through with that mug of yours, chump, it won't be temptin' any of my girls away! First off I'll slit that lyin' mouth of yours to ribbons."

"No, you won't!" Oliver said. He was on his feet now, his derringer in his hand.

McKelvey, swung around and stared. "I'll be damned! If it ain't a tooty-frooty in a cream puff suit. If you know what's good for you, boyo, you'll bugger off."

"Release that man, or I'll blow your ear off."

Sneering, McKelvey came at Oliver with the bottle. He fired and the thug yelped. He flopped on his back in the muck of the alley's surface drain, both hands pressed to the side of his face. Blood dripped between his fingers where the lobe of his right ear was shot away. "Jaysus!"

McKelvey pushed himself up on one elbow. "Get him, boys. He's only got one plug left in that sissy peashooter."

"True, but who wants to get it in the heart?" Oliver was considering how best to use his next and last shot when a night watchman's rattle cracked the taut silence.

"Blueboys!"

McKelvey's henchmen released Coy, grabbed their wounded leader by both arms and ran, half carrying and half dragging him with them.

As their racing feet drummed on the cobblestones, Coy dashed past Oliver. "Follow me if you don't want to end the night in the clink!"

A rag of cloud drifted over the moon, casting the alley into thicker shadow. Coy vaulted over a jumble of broken crockery. Oliver's boot caught on a fragment of plate and sent it ricocheting into the surface drain. At the other end of the alley the policeman's rattle clanged.

"Stop thief!" Feet clattered on the rough pavement.

Coy swerved through an open gate, hauled Oliver in after him and shoved it closed. The two men stood with their heaving chests pressed against the tall wooden barrier. Cloud left the moon long enough so that they looked into each other's faces. What sounded like a trio of policemen sped past.

As the hubbub of their pursuers receded, Coy whispered, "You're full of surprises, ain't you?"

"What's so surprising?"

"You could of beat it when those mugs got hold of me. Why didn't you?"

"I liked them less than I like you. Who are they?"

"McKelvy is a pimp. The other two run with him. He's after me 'cause I took one of his girls 'fore he had a chance to ruin her. McKelvy got hold of Maureen fresh off the boat when she didn't know no better. I put her straight and set her up in a decent job."

"I got the impression McKelvy would like to put you straight."

"He's longin' to bash me brains in, all right. Now he'd like to do the same for you. You made a bad enemy tonight, Redcastle. No one said you had to do it."

"That's right."

"I don't owe you a thing."

"Don't drag me into any more alleys, Coy."

"Then stay safe in yer bed. That's where lilies like you should be tuckin' their stems at night."

"You attacked because I was taking a walk in the dark?"

"I was doing me job, that's what. I'm paid to guard the bank nights, and you were hangin' 'round it." Coy stalked through the unfamiliar backyard and turned to the left. Oliver turned right and hurried home to change clothes.

CHAPTER THIRTEEN

B y midnight the sky had thickened to an inky sable, the hue of the pants and sweater Oliver had donned before leaving his house again that night.

As he made his way through the dark city, Doctor LeSane raced past on another night call. Did the poor man never sleep? Oliver crossed Lexington and saw a frowsy whore raising her skirt to tuck a drunken customer's money into her garter. In the lamp glow her mottled flesh looked bruised.

A few lights still winked at the Eutaw house, but the streets around it were placid. Carrying his leather bag full of cracksman's tools, he went to the back of the building where he was relieved to find an open door.

Several New England companies of Union veterans had banqueted that night. Holding his nose, he threaded a path past the leavings of the evening's meals--six-foot heaps of discarded crab and oyster shells, barrels containing the dismembered remains of hundreds of unlucky canvasback ducks, geese and rockfish.

As he slipped past the kitchen, he heard snatches of conversation from night workers grumbling as they labored over mountains of soiled crockery.

"Would you look at this filthy plate? What was he eating his damned duck with, a bayonet?"

Oliver climbed the backstairs to the second floor. Dim light oozed off sconces widely spaced on the walls. He opened his bag and took out his lock-pick tools. Seconds later the door to Sanders office swung open.

He lit the stub of a candle and crossed to the desk. He found the three files he wanted and extracted them. He'd just opened Enoch Rubman's when footsteps and muffled voices sounded in the hallway outside the door.

There was no place to hide save behind the heavy floor-to-ceiling curtains swathing the lone window. And those offered precious little cover.

He shoved his cracksman's case under the desk and dumped the files and other papers inside the false molding at the top of a large oak cabinet. He'd just slipped around the curtains when the door clicked open and heavy boots rang on the floor.

"I thought I left this door locked."

Oliver recognized Sanders voice.

"Do you smell candlewax?"

A match scratched and light flared.

"The night cleaners may have been in here. Anyway, what does it matter?" The second voice, distinctive because it was gravelly, sounded familiar. Oliver tried to place it.

"All right, gentlemen, the hour's late, so let's get down to business. Where do matters stand?" This was yet another voice, oozing assurance and also vaguely familiar.

Sanders again. "Two things. We need another partner, now that Rubman's out of the picture."

"A silent partner, preferably. Someone who can contribute money, but doesn't need to be put into the picture, if you take my meaning."

"A rich booby, in other words. All right, I'll see to that. And the other matter?"

"The date and time are set. Wednesday morning, June 22, while they're reviewing the parade. Gloger's our man, and we've picked his spot. Look here, this is candle wax on the desk. It wasn't there when I left."

"The cleaning people..."

"I've never known them to leave candle drippings."

A good twenty feet stood between Oliver's window and the ground. Directly below, he spied a dark mass he guessed might be the pile of oyster and crab pickings he'd held his nose for earlier. Gingerly, he tested the window's lock. It clicked into the open position with a metallic ping.

"Behind the curtain!"

As the three men lunged, Oliver shoved the window open. Yanking one of the draperies from its anchor, he pushed it at his assailants. Grabbing the other, he sailed out into the darkness. With a deafening rip, the cloth tore loose. He plummeted into a mountain of oyster shells.

Sixty shocked seconds ticked past before he began scratching his way through the shells.

"Here!" A hand seized his sweater and dragged him through the last of the garbage. "Get up on your feet, man. Any minute they'll be on the ground and after skinning you!"

CHAPTER FOURTEEN

"**S**hhh!" Coy pressed his ear to a crack in the shed where they'd taken shelter. Presently a tattoo of running feet leaked through it. "That's them," Coy whispered. "They're round the corner. "Let's beat it the other way."

"I can't."

"Want them yeggs to catch you?" Coy seized Oliver's arm and dragged him outside.

"Where are we going?" As he followed Coy, bits of razor sharp clamshell rained off him in a stinging snow. His face and hands ran blood. Thank God he hadn't broken any bones.

"You stink like a bucket of rotten fish!" Coy shoved him around a corner.

"Where are we going?"

"There's a fellow keeps a stable down here. He won't thank me for putrefying it with the likes of you. But you can hide there until morning. Who are those fellows chasing after you?"

"I'm not sure. Didn't get a good look at them."

"Musta' got a fair look at you to be wantin' your tail like that. Maybe it was one of them took a shot at you earlier."

On both scores, Oliver thought not. There'd been almost no light when he'd gone through the window, and the alley had been a pit of darkness. He hadn't seen their faces well enough to identify them, and he was certain they hadn't seen his. Until tonight, there'd been no reason why Sanders would want to kill him. Of course, when the man noticed the Rubman, Magruder and Nutwell files missing from his desk, he might put two and two together. Then there was the other question. What had Sanders and his pals been conspiring at and why had it involved a sharpshooter like Gloger? As Oliver pondered all this, he realized who had owned the other two familiar voices. Marshal Rackley and Edson Bailey.

Coy hissed, "Up to no good in there, were you?"

"On the contrary. I was doing a good deed."

"Yeah, yeah. You don't havta' tell me your business, and I don't havta' tell you mine.

"You told me yours. You're a night guard at the Monument National Bank, and you rescue damsels in distress from vicious pimps. In fact, you're a regular Sir Galahad, because now you've rescued me twice tonight."

Coy spat. "Enough of your japes!" He guided Oliver into an alley, opened a stable door and motioned him through. Inside, the air was warm, moist and thick with the comforting smell of horses, hay and leather. He lit an oil lamp hanging on a nail. Groaning, Oliver sank down onto a hay bale. Coy gazed at him, warring expressions chasing themselves across his tough young face.

"I'm damned if I know why I saved your bacon."

"Damned if I know, either." Oliver brushed a piece of shell from his chin, then appalled by the stink of his hands, looked around for a water bucket. "You must have followed me to the Eutaw House. Why?"

"Wanted to see what you were up to, all dressed in black like that. Figured you weren't going chimney sweeping."

"You trailed me home and then followed me again because you were afraid I might be going to rob your bank? C'mon man, do you take me for a fool?"

"It's part of me job to keep a lookout for suspicious characters. What were you up to? Thievery?"

He didn't answer and Coy shrugged. "I'll just use me fertile imagination on that question. All right then, be gone from here by mornin', and take your stink with you. I don't want to see you hanging around me bank again." He blew out the lamp, then opened the door and peered out before slipping through.

"One more thing," Oliver whispered.

"What's that?"

"Have you seen a tall man who wears a silver hunting watch with a big diamond mounted in it and a bullet dangling from the fob?"

"Why do you want to know?" Menace filtered into Coy's voice, menace that hadn't been there before.

"He's an old friend of mine."

"If I see him, I'll tell him you asked after his health. Sweet dreams." The door closed and Coy was gone.

"You slept late this mornin'. The early bird gets the worm." Mrs. Milawney topped up Oliver's glass of lemonade.

"I had a restless night." He lifted a strip of bacon to his mouth. A faint whiff of last night's adventure reached his nostrils and destroyed his appetite. Disgusted, he put it down. How many times would he have to bathe? Or was he going to smell rotting crabs forever?

Chloe sat across from him. She'd had her breakfast hours earlier, but had consented to nibble on a piece of toast while he finished his.

"I don't want to go visiting," she said.

Mrs. Milawney pushed a ringlet behind Chloe's ear. "Now, now, you mustn't be so shy, dearie. New friends are like silver in your pocket. I'm sure your papa's friends are very nice indeed."

"The lady is pretty," Chloe conceded. "But not as pretty as my mama."

Oliver sipped his coffee silently. It struck him that the two women did resemble each other, somewhat. Is that why he'd made a fool of himself with Marietta? All these years, had he been looking for Laura in other women and never finding his heart's desire? The thought did nothing to lighten his mood.

Later that afternoon he lifted Chloe out of a hired hack and set her slippered feet on the gravel road leading into the Singleton property.

"Their house is big," Chloe said.

"It is that." Oliver gazed at Zephyrus, the sprawling Greek style pillared mansion that had been in his mother's family for more than five generations. As a youngster, he'd persuaded his aunt to drive him past the place. After that, he'd found excuses to make his own way to Zephyrus so he could stand on the road and peer down its long gravel drive. It had looked so different from the rough little Kansas cabin where he'd grown up. At the time he'd cherished a fantasy that his grandfather would come out and invite him inside. That had never happened. When he'd visited his aunt his grandfather had ignored his presence in Baltimore. He'd never even caught a glimpse of the man.

Inside the mansion's black and white marble-paved entry, the old man's portrait gazed sternly down at him. While a servant went to summon his mistress, Oliver studied Andrew Singleton's austere features and found himself strangely shaken to see a face not unlike his own.

"Oliver! You've come! Oh, and you've brought your darling daughter!" Laura tripped into the hall in a cloud of pink silk and flowery scent.

After giving his shoulders a light squeeze, she turned to Chloe. The child stared at the floor, a forefinger in her mouth. Kneeling gracefully to bring their faces level, Laura exclaimed, "Oh, don't you look pretty! That's the loveliest straw sailor hat! And your ringlets! They're the most beautiful color!"

Laura took Chloe's hand. "Come out to the garden. We have got a croquet game all set up and the loveliest tea cakes and wintergreen juice. There's a swing, too!"

He trailed the two females down a center hall, catching glimpses of rooms richly furnished in mahogany slippery with horsehair and hard tapestry. Oil paintings with ornate gilt frames paved the walls. He smelled beeswax and the faint, not unpleasant odor of decaying wood.

In this house, his mother had grown up. It was impossible not to measure the luxury surrounding her girlhood against the rough farmstead in which she'd raised him and his brothers. When Rosemary Singleton had eloped with Tucker Redcastle, an abolitionist preacher who'd visited Baltimore on a speaking tour with Frederick Douglas, she'd cut herself off from her wealthy family. Oliver had never seen her in a silky dress like the one Laura wore. Between his father's hopeless farming and the rigors of the wilderness where they'd homesteaded, they'd been so poor that there were times when he and his brothers had gone shoeless.

Laura led them into a solarium filled with exotic plants. A rainbow of birds twittered from cages hung from potted trees. When Chloe caught sight of a green and gold parrot, her mouth dropped open.

The solarium's glass doors opened onto a garden. Beyond it a meadow sloped to a pond. The afternoon sun sparkled on the water, making of it a bright blue eye in a carpet of smooth green.

"Come and say hello to Griff. He's dying to speak to you."

"Is he?"

Laura slapped his forearm lightly. "Of course, he is! You men are so silly! Now come on along."

They found Griff sitting under a trellis loaded with leathery grape leaves. At the crunch of their feet on the gravel path, he turned his head. Shock stopped Oliver's breath. Griff's hair, what remained of it, had turned completely white. Round dark glasses on wire frames shielded his eyes. His fleshless face and body looked like an old man's. Then he smiled and Oliver glimpsed some of the debonair young man he had hero-worshipped.

"Olly! Griff drawled, "you've sprouted into a giant. You block out the sun." He held out his hand.

Grasping it, Oliver tested the long thin bones beneath the papery skin. "Then you can see me."

"I'm not completely blind. I can make out your outline. It's just the details I lack. It's been a long time since we were boys roaming the harbor, eh?"

CHAPTER FIFTEEN

The table where the four of them lounged enjoyed a fine view of the meadow below. A servant had brought them pitchers of iced drinks and a tray piled high with tiny cucumber sandwiches and candied orange slices.

"Chloe darling, join me in a game of croquet," Laura wheedled. "It'll be such fun!"

At first Chloe refused, but Laura persisted until they made their way down the hill. Alone with Griff, Oliver listened to the rustle of the wind stirring the yew branches behind them. Memories crowded his mind.

"I'm sorry," Griff said.

"Sorry?"

Griff stared straight ahead. "After the war, I never wrote to you. I should have done, I know. I thought of it often, and Laura suggested it, too. But I never did. Blame it on this." He pointed at his dark glasses.

"What happened to your eyes?"

"Partial blindness, a legacy left me by Point Lookout."

"I've heard stories about that prison camp." It was difficult for Oliver to imagine his aristocratic cousin in such a place. Griff had always been so persnickety about his clothes, his food, his boots, his horses.

His mouth twisted. "I and fifty other unlucky souls arrived at Point Lookout in the summer of '63."

"Did you know each other?"

"Only six others from Warren's."

Oliver nodded. Griff had fought with a Virginia Company, Warren's Light Infantry of Front Royal.

 "We were a pitiful group," he continued, "ragged, half-starved, some of us even lacking shoes. I spent my first night in a tent with twenty other men. We slept arranged like spokes in a wagon wheel, our feet touching. They explained to me that it was, 'Root, Pig, or die.'" He laughed harshly. "Bad water and the food, what little there was of it, worse. Surviving the Point meant cultivating a taste for week-old table scraps and learning how to trap and cook rats for your supper.

"That first night six of the men in my tent died of dysentery. I woke up next to a stone cold body. Imagine what it's like seeing a corpse staring at you from no more than a hand's breadth."

"But your eyes. . ."

"A common ailment at the Point. Glare on the sand, the white tents and the water surrounding the tents caused temporary blindness. Most men recovered once they left the camp. I didn't, even after I escaped."

"You escaped the camp?"

"It was after something particularly vile occurred. One of the prisoners threw a brick that wounded a Negro guard on the palisades. When nobody would tattle on who threw the brick, the Union officer in charge cut out a hundred men and ordered them to stand in the wind until they told who did it. It still gives me nightmares."

"The war still gives us all nightmares."

"True enough, but this was something wonderful. Picture the dead of winter, one of the coldest nights of the year. The wind was like a knife. Half the men, who'd been chosen for punishment purely at random, didn't have shoes or even a jacket. Most were already weak from starvation and sickness. By morning twenty were dead. After that five of us decided we'd sooner die than continue in that evil hole."

"It couldn't have been easy to escape the place."

"If you were caught you'd be shot at the dead line for trying, or hung up by the thumbs. We didn't care. It was get out or join the fellas in the peach orchard, which is what we called the graveyard adjacent to the camp. Many times I watched them shoveling bodies under it stacked like cordwood."

"How'd you go about escaping?"

Griff folded his hands in the lap of his white trousers. The trill of Laura's and Chloe's laughter drifted across the lawn.

He said quietly, "After roll call, we crept as near the dead line as possible. As the sentinels met and separated, we made a dash for freedom."

Oliver pictured the scene. The camp would have been shrouded in winter darkness. The half-starved men would have been desperate.

"I'll never forget the feel of the rocks in the sand stinging my bare feet as I ran," Griff said. "A deep inlet patrolled by cavalry flowed from the river to the bay. We ran to the bay point about two hundred and fifty yards from the beach and waded out to a sand shoal. It was dark as Eurebus and colder than an ice-house in January, but we managed to keep on that shoal and wade out until it got so deep that two of us froze and drowned. Cavalry pickets shot the rest. I was the only one who got through."

"After that?"

"After that, I bushwacked a Union soldier, stole his uniform and made my way back to Laura. I arrived a physical wreck. If not for my eyes, I would have rejoined my company. The partial blindness along with my frostbitten feet made that impossible. So, I've been here ever since." His lips twisted.

"You're a lucky man."

"I am." Griff nodded his agreement. "A couple of fellas who'd been captured with me were among that group of men punished for throwing the brick. Zack Primm and Frank Wisbey."

"Men who fought with Warren's?"

Griff nodded. "Zack and Frank came around to visit yesterday. They're with the thirty Front Royals who've journeyed up from Virginia for the encampment. They said almost everyone I knew when I was at Lookout died before the end. If it wasn't dysentery and diarrhea, it was typhoid fever, scurvy and the itch.

And when it wasn't sickness, it was a minie ball shot at random by a Union guard on night patrol."

"They would shoot into the tents when they were on night patrol?"

"Happened all the time." Griff turned his face toward Laura's voice, carried like the tinkle of faraway bells on the summer breeze. She'd just sent a red croquet ball rocketing through a pair of wickets and was urging Chloe to do the same with her green ball. Chloe's ball struck the goal post and she shrieked with joy.

"All of us who went off to that war were ignorant children," Griff murmured. "We thought we were marching to glory when really we were marching to death. If it didn't put us in a grave, it maimed our bodies or killed our souls. None of us came back unscathed."

A fat bee dived past his head and hovered over a clump of white aconite. Its buzz made Oliver think of the insects gathering over the bodies in the fields at Antietam. Some of the corn stalks had been sticky with blood. It had been hot that day, too.

Apparently, the whirr of the bee's wings had stirred a similar recollection in Griff. He said, "There were twenty thousand men at Point Lookout when I was there, many of them boys of fourteen, fifteen and sixteen. Children."

Both men fell silent, assailed by memories of war. Finally, Griff said, "I've talked about myself. What about you, Olly? I hear that after Lee signed that damned traitorous peace treaty you became a lawman."

"I've worked for the Pinkerton Agency. That's finished. I'm here in Baltimore to try my hand at a new business. Or at least, I will be when I've handled a last case. Chloe needs a settled life."

"Ah. Laura tells me you are a widower. Where did you meet Chloe's mother?"

"In New York. She was an actress." Oliver didn't explain that they hadn't been married, though the news was bound to get out. Mrs. Milawney had already guessed.

Laura and Chloe trudged up the hill, swinging their croquet

mallets. Oliver stared at his daughter. Her face glowed from exercise. He'd never seen her look so healthy or so happy.

Laura gave the child a squeeze. "Oh, you are a wonder, you beautiful girl baby!" She shot Oliver a wink. "Your little darling beat me. I think she has her daddy's unerring aim. You must bring her again soon so I'll have a chance to even the score."

Chloe gazed adoringly back at Laura. When he called her name and she turned her face to his, her smile faded. A few minutes later, he rose to leave. As he shook his cousin's hand, he asked, "By the way, I mentioned earlier that I'm working on a last case. As it happens, it involves a man named Ben Magruder who served at Point Lookout. Is the name familiar?"

Griff's hand dropped out of Oliver's. He said, "I'll never forget that name as long as I live. Magruder was the Union officer who ordered me and ninety-nine other innocent men to spend a winter night freezing to death."

CHAPTER SIXTEEN

"**M**iss Kinchman, I presume." Beacher Penrose blocked his doorway. He was a tall, slender man with black hair and long, delicate hands. For a split second Hannah was shaken. It might have been Gilbert standing there.

"Come in, come in. Let' have a look at you. I'm anxious to get to work."

As he shut the door behind her, Hannah tore her gaze away from him. He wasn't Gilbert, of course, but he looked so much like him. The same marble brow and long lashes.

She looked about the huge room with a feeling close to agoraphobia. Rivers of light flooded through a bank of tall windows. It fell in buttery puddles on chunks of half shaped marble, alabaster and limestone. Stained and spattered drop-cloths glowed on the floor.

Several large portrait easels stood in shadow. Stacks of canvases in rolls and on stretchers had been shoved carelessly into corners. On a low table Hannah saw drills, saws, planers. A strong smell of turpentine and marble dust flavored the air.

"I particularly requested a thin woman." Penrose's chin rested in one cupped hand. His large amber eyes mapped Hannah's form critically.

Beneath his gray smock, striped trousers and gaiters, his form appeared long-legged and graceful. As he shifted his weight from foot to foot, he reminded Hannah of a restive gazelle sniffing something on the air he didn't quite like and preparing for flight.

She replied to his remark mildly. "All my life people have told me that I am too thin. The woman who engaged me to model for you seemed to think I was just what you had ordered."

"Is that so? We shall see. Disrobe, please." He pointed at a folding screen set up at one end of the room. It was painted with chipped images of gypsies. "You'll find a robe hung over a chair. You may put it on when you've removed your clothes."

Behind the screen, Hannah saw a small table with a glass and pitcher of water, a chair and a chamber pot. She folded her dress and laid it over the chair. It was a warm summer day, but as she removed her camisole and unhooked her corset, her fingers felt cold.

This was not the first time Hannah had worked as an artist's model. Twice before, once in Chicago and once in Philadelphia, she'd been between theater jobs and down to her last few pennies. She'd remedied her situation by stripping for art students. It had been easier than she'd imagined. Hannah was not ashamed of her neat, smooth body. And that's all she'd been to the students, a body.

There had been anonymity in that experience. This time would be different. She would be alone with Penrose who reminded her of her runaway husband. She had always been attracted to men with his type of Byronic male beauty--men who would ultimately let her down. Like Gilbert, who'd emptied her purse to run off with another actress. She sighed and stepped out of her bustle. Then she began untying the strings on her drawers.

"What's taking you so long? Hurry it up?" Penrose's voice shot through the screen like a bolt from a crossbow.

"Do you want me to remove my shoes?"

"Of course. I plan to sculpt a nymph. Nymphs aren't in the habit of wearing button-ups."

Hannah rolled down her lisle stockings and reached for the silk robe he had provided. She drew it closed, conscious of its sensuous caress against her naked breasts and calves.

As she stepped around the screen, she felt the shock of the bare wood floor against the pads of her toes. It was gritty with dust and almost hot from sunlight. Penrose sat in the center of the room placing quick charcoal strokes into a sketchbook. "Now let's have a look at you. Drop the robe, please."

The robe slithered to the floor. Shy despite herself, Hannah avoided his glance. She struggled not to bring her hands up to her breasts. When she did meet his eyes, his expression shocked her. His thin nostrils quivered. He looked disgusted.

"Your breasts are much too large."

Hannah blinked. Her breasts would hardly overflow a moustache cup. All her adult life she been told that they were much too small.

Penrose had turned away as if he couldn't bear to look at her. "I've a commission to sculpt a nymph for a rich man's garden. Nymphs are delicate creatures with small, graceful limbs. They do not possess gross dangling breasts, nor round bellies and great chunks of thighs. They do not have. . ." He hesitated.

Mortified by the term "chunky" applied to thighs which she knew were almost as slim and athletic as a boy's, Hannah waited to hear what nymphs did not have.

"Hair," Penrose spit out in a disgusted whisper.

"Do you want me to leave?"

Penrose tapped his stick of charcoal against his lip. "No, no. You're the least objectionable of the three they've sent me. Put the robe back on, please."

When she had complied, he showed her the sketch he had been making. "Do you think you can get yourself into that position and stay in it for twenty minutes at a time?"

The sketch showed a kneeling figure folded over itself like a squeezebox. The hands and forearms were flat on the ground, the head raised. "I don't know."

"I'll spread a blanket for you. You needn't hold your head up like that until I tell you. And make sure that your breasts are hidden by your arms and legs, please."

Hannah did her best to comply. With her legs crimped up under her chest and her head buried in her arms, she felt rather like a frog. Still, it was not as uncomfortable as she had feared, and it gave her an illusion of privacy.

It also gave her an opportunity to think. She had come here to learn more about Penrose. She had anticipated an older man, and one far less comely. Peeping through her fingers, she admired his profile with its high cheekbones and long, narrow nose. Yet how very odd was his prudish reaction to the sight of her naked body. Surely a sculptor must be a man accustomed to female nudity.

The room grew quiet. Except for the strokes of Penrose's charcoal on paper, only the occasional jingle of harness and creak of carriage wheels on the street outside drifted through the window. Warm light bathed Hannah's bare buttocks and heated the backs of her heels. She was half asleep when the touch of Penrose's fingers on the nape of her neck startled her.

"No, don't move. Stay as you are. I'm taking the pins out of your hair."

She felt the subtle tug of a pin sliding against her skull. As the hair rolled up tightly at the back of her head loosened, she forced herself to relax. Penrose's hands were gentle and slow. One by one the pins came sliding from their living silken cushion. Coils of hair sagged and then slid sensuously around her shoulders and over her back.

She felt his long fingers comb through the hair. As they brushed her back and flicked her sides, she could not keep herself from shuddering.

"The nymph I plan to sculpt," he whispered, "is to be an abandoned little creature, a force of nature unconstrained by human conventions. Her hair must express her wildness."

Penrose stepped back and recommenced his sketches. As the afternoon progressed, he circled Hannah's naked body many times, sketching her from every angle. Listening to the slow brush of his feet on the wood floor, she visualized a leisurely panther stalking prey. Beneath her unclad belly, her tightly pleated legs had fallen asleep.

"I can't remain in this position any longer."

"Very well. Get up when I leave the room. You may have a quarter of an hour to refresh yourself."

Hannah heard the door click and raised her head. When she had restored enough circulation to get to her feet she reached for the robe.

After that, she stretched her limbs and then poured herself a glass of water. Sipping it, she wandered about the studio, staring at the objects furnishing it. They were all beautiful. The chunks of stone, sculpted by light, had a stark loveliness.

Hannah drifted over to the canvases stacked with their fronts against the wall. Picking through them, she saw landscapes and figures in chaotic swirls of color and shape. A portrait of a naked young woman caught her eye. She turned the canvas to get a better look.

The figure, slender and flat-chested as a boy, was very lifelike. Hannah might have thought that the model really was a young boy if it weren't for the rich brown hair piled atop her head and banded with artificial flowers. Tiny curls framed her delicate face.

Behind Hannah, the door clicked. Penrose entered the room and stopped short. "I don't remember giving you permission to examine my canvases."

"My curiosity got the better of me. I'm sorry."

"If I wish to display my work to the public, I give out invitations."

"Since I doubt I will ever receive such an invitation, I can't regret that I've seen this portrait. The work is very fine and the subject is exceedingly beautiful." Hannah turned the painting back to the wall.

When the portrait was out of sight and Hannah had stepped away from it, Penrose said, "That was my wife, Flora. I finished painting her just before she died."

Hannah was surprised and a little shocked that he had painted his wife naked. She said, "I'm sorry to hear that you have lost your wife. You must be glad that you have her portrait."

"Not in the least," he replied savagely. "I hate the sight of it."

CHAPTER SEVENTEEN

"**A**LLAN ILL. CAN'T DELIVER INFORMATION AT THIS TIME."

Oliver stuffed the telegram from Allan Pinkerton's wife into his vest pocket. If Allan couldn't answer a question about a possible assassin, he must be sick as a poisoned cat. It sounded as if he'd never read the damn telegram.

Should I wire one of his boys, Oliver wondered. If he was being hunted, it was better to know sooner rather than later.

He fired off a telegram to William and sent another to Allan, this time expressing concern about his health and inquiring about Mrs. Hannah Kinchman.

Next, he stopped in at Edson Bailey's bank. It was a solid gray stone establishment with weathered brass doors. Inside, the polished granite floor and reverential hush made Oliver think of a church. Only whispered voices and the rustle of money broke the silence.

When he asked to speak with Mr. Bailey, the clerk raised his eyebrows. A moment later the young man came out from behind a thick oak door with a changed demeanor. "Mr. Bailey will see you now. Please follow me."

Bailey's office was furnished and carpeted as befit a man of his importance. Looking far more impressive behind his massive desk than he had in Bombick's gym, he rose and extended his hand.

"Glad to see you, Redcastle. The more I hear of you, the better you sound."

"Who've you been talking to?"

Bailey opened his humidor and offered a cigar which Oliver refused. "Our good Marshal Rackley speaks highly of you, as does Bombick. He tells me you've come into a nice inheritance and settled in our fair city to stay. I'm pleased to hear it. We need up and coming men in Baltimore."

Bailey returned to his desk and wrote out a check for one hundred dollars. "Take it with my thanks for services rendered."

"I appreciate the gesture, but Marshal Rackley already paid me. I didn't come here to hold you up for more money."

"Then why did you come?"

"For advice. I'd like to invest some funds in a likely enterprise. But when it comes to business, I'm a novice. You know how money flows in the city. I'm hoping you'll give me a tip."

Pointing Oliver to a chair next to a polished brass spittoon, Bailey asked, "What investment possibilities have you looked into?"

"So far, only two. I've talked to a glover eager to sell what he claims is a steady living, and I've had discussions with a local scientist named Remsen. He's developed a formula for an artificial sweetener that may have commercial value. Saccharin I think he calls it."

"Gloves, artificial sweeters." Bailey waved a dismissive hand. "Those are either penny-ante or fly-by-night. A man of your stripe wants something that will make real money. I happen to be assisting a group of prominent local citizens who are pooling their resources to take advantage of such a deal. They're looking for one or two more silent partners. Sound interesting?"

"Very. But I'd need to know the details."

Polite knuckles rattled on Bailey's door. The clerk stuck his head in. "Marshal Rackley to see you, sir."

"Speak of the devil, send him in."

Rackley swept into the room, his short legs moving with great energy. Despite the June heat, he wore full official regalia of double breasted blue wool suit studded with brass buttons. Tucked under one meaty arm, he carried his marshal's helmet.

"I've got the agreements," he announced in his raspy voice and tossed a tightly rolled scroll of paper onto the banker's large desk. Seeing Oliver, Rackley stopped short.

"I was just offering Mr. Redcastle here my thanks," Bailey explained. "What do you think, Rackley? Mr. Redcastle here says he is looking for an investment opportunity."

Rackley spit copiously into the spittoon. "What sort of opportunity would that be?"

"Something lucrative. Something like the deal Mr. Bailey says he's working on with a group of prominent citizens. I gather you're one of those citizens, Marshal?"

There was a long silence. Oliver felt the hair at the back of his neck lift. Was the deal between Bailey and Rackley connected, as he suspected, with the conspiracy he had stumbled into at the Eutaw House? What was it about and where had Enoch Rubman fit in?

Rackley asked, "What sort of money are you talking about investing?"

Oliver named a sum considerably larger than the amount available to him.

Rackley's brows lifted. "A grand amount of money is required to bring off this deal. We've already got most of what we need safe in Bailey's vaults. But we could sweeten the pot. If you're really interested, I'll jaw with my other partners and get back to you."

"I'm interested if the odds seem right," Oliver said, "but I need to have some idea what this is about. Can't you at least give me a hint?"

Bailey tore a corner from a letter on his desk and wrote one word on it. He slid the scrap of paper across to Oliver who read it. The word Bailey had written was "nautical."

"Not much to go on."

Bailey shrugged. "It'll give you something to think about while we're deciding whether to give you more."

A few minutes later Oliver walked out of the bank and turned right. The display window next to the bank caught his eye. Wiley's Fine Import Wines and Spirits. It was the same wine shop he'd noticed the night of his escapade at The Eutaw House. He stood for several minutes mulling over the conversation he'd just had inside the bank. At the same time, he admired the attractive array of French vintages in the shop window. He was considering going into the place when Marshal Rackley's heavy hand descended onto his shoulder.

"What's this I hear about you working for Garrett up at the B&O?"

Oliver explained that he was investigating the accident which had killed Rubman, Magruder and Nutwell.

Rackley frowned. "I thought you were quits with the Pinkertons. Are you setting up a detecting agency? Because I don't mind telling you, Redcastle, I don't relish having a private citizen sticking his nose into Baltimore's police matters. Fact is, I won't tolerate it."

"Your people consider those men's deaths accidental. Garrett hired me to make sure, that's all."

Rackly continued to look suspicious. "What have you found out?"

"Not much. Right now I'm looking for a stranger in town, a tall man, well dressed, wears a silver hunting case watch studded with a big diamond and decorated with a gold-plated minie ball. You wouldn't have seen him by any chance?"

"In case you haven't noticed, Baltimore is full of strangers these days. There are delegations of 'em falling all over each other. You haven't answered my question. Are you planning to set up as a detective?"

"I agreed to help Garrett, but that's my swan song. I want to go into a business that has nothing to do with crooks and murderers." Oliver smiled. "I've always liked the water. Something nautical would suit me."

The suspicion eased from Rackley's gaze. "After you left the bank, Bailey and I talked. We like the notion of having you as our business partner."

"Then you're going to tell me what this deal you're cooking

up is all about?"

"First we'd like you to meet some of our other associates and get their opinions."

"This is beginning to sound more like a social club than a business deal."

"Men who are doing serious business together need to get along. These fellas are all sportsmen, so let's make it a sporting occasion. What do you think of a shooting match between you and my man Gloger?"

Oliver didn't think much of it at all. But he nodded and smiled. "Name the date."

In the wee hours of the next morning Oliver slipped up the backstairs of the Eutaw House. He planned to revisit Sanders' office and retrieve the file folders he'd hidden.

He made his way down the dimly lit corridor leading to the office. The hotel, full up with out-of-town veterans, felt like a hive of sleeping bees.

Someone coughed and then cleared his throat. Oliver froze. He peered around a corner that formed a slight jog in the corridor. Some twenty yards away a thickset man sat dozing in a chair set squarely in front of Sanders' office door. Sanders and his crew had posted a guard to make sure there were no more break-ins.

Oliver stood fuming then silently made his way back toward the stairs. Outside in the moonlight, he stared up at Sanders' office window. The wall of the hotel, with its balconies and fancy brickwork, offered quite a few footholds. A skilled climber with the right tools might be able to scale it. A few years back Oliver would have considered trying it himself. Now, with his ailing knee, he knew that was impossible. "Damnation!" he muttered. The file folders in Sanders office, if they were even still where he'd secreted them, would have to wait.

CHAPTER EIGHTEEN

Two-dozen veterans of the Warren Light Infantry of Front Royal Virginia milled in the Eutaw House lobby. It was strange to see them dressed in their butternut uniforms. It was even stranger to see an Ohio delegation dressed in Union blue shaking their hands and slapping their backs. That night the Ohioans were escorting the Confederate veterans to a dinner at Barnums.

When Oliver asked for Primm and Wiseby, one of the Royals told him, "They've slipped out with some other fellas to a place called Kernan's."

Oliver remembered Kernan's from his boyhood. It was a rowdy spot, a combination drinking hall and low class theater. In the old days he and Griff had liked to sneak in there to see the girl performers in their revealing outfits.

A half hour later he walked into the place. It hadn't changed. Above the reek of beer, hard liquor and cigar smoke, the rafters pulsed with ribald shouts, cat-calls and applause from men watching "Aimee, The Human Fly." The performer, dressed in spangled pink tights and black gauze wings, walked head down above the drunken onlookers. In between deep gulps from their tankards, they leered up at her bobbling breasts.

On the lookout for Primm and Wiseby, Oliver spotted John L. Sullivan, surrounded as before by a knot of loud admirers. Sullivan caught his eye and raised his mug of ale in a friendly mock salute. "Give that old bastard Bombick my regards!"

"I'll do that!"

Primm had been described as a short man with a handlebar moustache and Wiseby as bald with a thick red beard. Oliver found the two Confederate veterans at a table in the middle of the hall. They were with six others in Confederate uniforms. This might have been unwise in another northern city over-flowing with Union veterans. But Baltimore was a town with strong southern sympathies. Griff Singleton was typical of the town's old aristocracy, most of whom had gone sesesh, too.

Oliver introduced himself to Wiseby as Griff's cousin. Beaming, the bearded man invited him to take a seat.

"Don't recall old Griff ever speaking of you," Wiseby said after Oliver had filled a glass from the pitcher being passed around the table.

"Maybe that's because I fought with McClellan until Lincoln fired him."

Conversation stopped. "Swear I know that fella' from some-where," a beery voice shouted.

The remark had come from a bald man with a straw colored moustache. He looked vaguely familiar, but Oliver couldn't place him. He turned back to Wiseby and Primm.

"What made you go with the Federals?" Primm asked.

"My family was butchered by Quantrill in his raid on Law-rence." Oliver had declared for the Union before Quantrill's in-famous raid, and he'd done it against his parents wishes.

Primm grimaced. "War was hard on all of us, I reckon."

Wiseby said, "Primm and me, we're here instead of banquet-ing at Barnum's with the rest of the Royals because we couldn't stomach being treated to a feed by a bunch of Federals. You'd feel the same if you'd spent time at Point Lookout like we did."

Oliver nodded. "Griff told me about the place."

"Griff wouldn't have told you the half of it," Wiseby retorted gruffly. "Too much the gent. Sad what's happened to him. It's a funny thing. Of all those who tried escaping from Lookout that night, he's the only one made it. Yet seems like it took all the stuffings out of him."

Oliver was curious to hear Wiseby's version of Griff's escape. "What happened?"

"Somehow, old Magruder must have got wind of the scheme, for when those boys tried to run for it the guards were lying in wait. Griff was damned lucky to escape, half blind the way he was. Too bad he never recovered his sight. He's got a right good looking wife. A shame he can't appreciate her."

"You don't need to see a woman to appreciate her," Primm pointed out with a leer.

A girl slid from the roof to the stage and a roar of surprise and approval exploded from the crowd. Clenched in her teeth she held a string attached to a wheel on a wire.

Ignoring a flea-bitten terrier which trod over his feet, Oliver said, "You mentioned the name Magruder. A couple of weeks back a man named Ben Magruder was killed in a train accident."

"The bastard's dead?" Wiseby spat onto the littered floor and watched his spittle sink into sawdust and peanut shells. "Praise the lord!"

According to Wiseby and Primm, Magruder had been a conscienceless, sadist and inept to boot. "We didn't get into Baltimore until a couple of days after that accident," Primm said. "And we're the only two left of the Front Royals who were in Lookout and knew what a son of a bitch Magruder was--other than your cousin, that is. Magruder used to like to pick on him. Drug him regular up to the guard house."

Primm was shouting over the noise of the crowd, which had been getting steadily more raucous. A fist-fight had broken out near the stage where a couple of drunken patrons had tried to get a closer look at the girl with the iron teeth. Oliver watched an inebriated man weave past and then crash headfirst into a nearby table.

Distracted by the confusion, Oliver jumped when someone thumped rudely on his shoulder. It was the man with the straw colored moustache. "Knew I'd seen you before," he snarled. "You were a damned Union spy."

Staring, into his furious face, Oliver was cast back twenty years. He'd met Allan Pinkerton through General McClellan.

When Pinkerton had set up his network of spies to go south, McClellan had recommended Oliver as "a young man who can handle a gun and use his fists." Pinkerton had taken him on.

His first assignment had been to play driver to Harry Barnett. Capitalizing on Harry's fancy English accent, Pinkerton had dressed him in a stovepipe hat, the latest English-cut clothes, and provided a coach loaded with cases of champagne.

Harry's cover story had been that he was an English gentleman on a grand tour of the south. For nineteen days the two young men had toured the Rebel lines, uncorking their champagne with Rebel commanders. They'd returned with detailed reports of fortifications, troop numbers, arms and provisions.

"You lying bastard!" the man with the corn colored moustache shouted.

"What are you blatherin' about, Pailer?" Wiseby demanded.

Pailer. The name struck a chord. Oliver realized he'd met the man with the corn colored moustache behind southern lines when he'd had a full head of golden hair. He'd been Colonel Patton's adjutant.

"This man and a fella dressed up in fancy duds and talkin' like a Englishman with a lemon in his mouth spent three days swilling champagne with Patton. They bamboozled him into thinkin' they was British nobles on a tour. After they cozened him into showing them everything about our position, they came back with Cox and whupped us at Coal Mouth. Some of my best pards got blowed to smithereens because of this lying Yankee spy."

An ugly growl went up from the other men at the table.

Wiseby demanded, "Redcastle, how come I don't hear you denying what Pailer says?"

"I told you I fought for the Union. For God's sake, man, the war has been over for twenty years."

Judging from the fury gathering on the other men's faces, they'd forgotten that. Oliver stood. Before he could escape, Pailer, cursing, seized the sleeve of his jacket. Oliver kicked his assailant's legs out from under him and heard the fabric of his sleeve tear as the other man went down.

Screaming with rage, Wiseby launched himself across Pailer's fallen body. While Oliver fought to beat the big Virginian off, chaos erupted on every side.

It was as if the entire hall, which had been simmering with drink and bottled up memories of the war, had reached a boiling point. Men in bits and pieces of Union and Confederate uniform who'd been sharing jokes minutes earlier, tore at each other. A waiter dumped a tray of overflowing pitchers over the heads of a dozen men thrashing around him. Shots went off and the girl dangling from the high wire over the stage opened her mouth to scream and fell into the waiter and the churning men. Tables crashed to the floor, sending shards of broken beer glasses flying into the crowd. Somewhere in the din, a police whistle hooted.

Oliver managed to bring his knee up hard into Wiseby's groin. As his grip loosened, Oliver shoved his elbow into the Virginian's belly and pushed him back at Primm. Kicking his way free of Pailer, who snatched at his pantlegs, he scrambled over the fallen table behind him. Dodging a flying tankard, he skirted another table in hopes of eluding two other Confederates who were trying to pursue him through the writhing melee.

A total stranger slammed a fist into his stomach. As he went down, he rolled under a chair in hopes of avoiding the stranger's booted foot. The chair toppled over him, and he saw John L. Sullivan seize the pugnacious brawler's collar and shove him reeling into the crowd. Sullivan had removed his jacket and rolled up his sleeves to reveal brawny forearms. Smiling, he waded into the melee.

A police whistled shrilled. An arm seized his and dragged him out from under the chair.

CHAPTER NINETEEN

Penrose cleared his throat. "You're the most silent model I've ever engaged."

"Really?" With her hair and hands covering her face, Hannah's voice sounded as if it were issuing from a tiny dark cave. This was her third modeling session with Penrose. So far she'd learned nothing.

"You seem different from the others. It's made me curious about you"

"In what way." She tried not to let her shoulders tense.

"It's clear from the manner in which you speak and dress that you've had some education. Yet you do not exhibit any ridiculous female modesty where your body is concerned. That's unusual in a woman of your class."

"You're mistaken about my class, as you put it. I was raised in a three-room farmhouse, the only girl in a family of older brothers. Why should bodily matters embarrass me? We all have bodies. It's just nature."

"Your husband is a fortunate man."

"My husband deserted me. I haven't heard from him in years."

"Ah. Has he broken your heart?"

Hannah considered that. When she had married Gilbert she had been so in love with him that sometimes, looking at him, she felt actual pain in the region of her heart. He was so different from the rough men she'd grown up with.

After they were married he had seemed to want her to be

more of a mother to him than a lover. But, charmed by his eloquent tongue and graceful manners, she hadn't minded. She had been willing to work for him and coddle his whims. When he left her, she had thought she might die.

"Yes," she answered Beacher's question. "My husband broke my heart."

"Has no man ever taken his place?"

"Not yet."

There was a period of silence. Then Beacher said in a voice filled with sadness, "I loved my beautiful wife, too. Insanely. No woman will ever replace her in my heart. I am inconsolable."

Redcastle, you're like an onion in a stew, always smack dab in the thick of things." Marshal Rackley jabbed his nightstick into Oliver's back, urging him onto the street. Several skirmishes had broken out on the cobblestones in front of Kernan's. Youngsters from the neighborhood were throwing rocks. While Sergeant Kanary of the Eastern and his men waded in with saps and clubs to deal with the ruckus, Rackley pointed at a police wagon. Oliver joined the marshal on the driver's bench where Rackley demanded, "Now, who kicked over the bee hive?"

When Oliver explained, Rackley shook his head. "I didn't like it when Garrett told me you were investigating this railroad bang-up for him. I was thinking then there'd be trouble."

They watched a couple of police prod a half dozen battered patrons out onto the cobblestones. Oliver said, "You can't cram a horde of Union and Confederate veterans into a beer hall and not expect a dust-up."

Rackley shrugged, the double row of brass buttons on his coat winking in the street lamp. "We've been expectin' trouble from the hour we heard about this encampment folly. Were you telling me the truth? Will this job with Garrett be your last?"

"Definitely."

In front of them, the team of horses wheezed and stamped their feet. One of them sent a spray of hot urine hissing onto the cobblestones.

"All right, then," Rackley said. "I'll take you at your word. Still willing to give Gloger a shooting match when you meet with my investor's group?"

"Any time."

"How does Wednesday sound?"

When Oliver nodded, Rackley spat over the side of the wagon. "As long as you don't plan to become a permanent thorn in my side, I'm thinking I don't mind giving you a tip. You know the man you described to me?"

"The man with the diamond studded watch and gold bullet?"

"That's the one. He's been seen talking to a blackamoor who lives in Fells Point, name of Charlie Douglas. He's Frederick Douglas's grandson." Rackley snorted. "He plays the fiddle."

"I appreciate the information."

"Don't go forgetting," Rackley warned, "this is your last detecting job. For the time being, I'm your friend and maybe your business partner. Sooner or later everything that happens in this town gets to my ear. Lie to me, interfere with me, try to cheat me, and I'll be the worst enemy you ever had."

Aurelia Burnside Davies, Flora Penrose's older sister, lived in a narrow brick house on Montgomery Street in Federal Hill. Before knocking on Mrs. Davies door, Hannah had learned that Mrs. Davies, ten years older than the ill-fated Flora, was a widow who'd never remarried. Her young husband had been killed late in the war. Having acquired nursing skills caring for Confederate prisoners at Fort McHenry, Mrs. Davies had carried those skills on at a local hospital where she was now a head nurse.

Hannah had thought that Mrs. Davies might resemble her sister. But when the widow opened her door, she looked nothing like the elfin, flat-chested creature in Beacher Penrose's painting. She was a sturdy woman with an ample bosom, snapping brown eyes, a no-nonsense manner and an untidy bun of dark brown hair liberally threaded with gray.

After Hannah introduced herself, Mrs. Davies looked her up

and down. "I don't understand what it is you want."

"I'd like to talk to you about your sister. I'm an old school friend of Flora's. We attended Miss Selden's academy together."

"Really?"

"May I come in?"

"You've come at an inopportune moment, Mrs. Kinchman. I was just on my way to the hospital."

"I won't take much of your time. I promise."

"Oh very well, but I won't be able to offer you tea and there's nothing in the house that even faintly resembles cake or cookies."

"I don't require tea or cookies." Hannah followed Mrs. Davies up a narrow staircase to a tiny sitting room. The curtains at its solitary window were drawn, casting its threadbare furniture into deep shadow. As Hannah walked into it, she felt the trembling in the pit of her stomach go quiet. It was always like that before she gave a performance. When she'd knocked on Mrs. Davies door she'd been almost sick with stage fright. Now that the performance had begun, she felt calm.

"What is it you want?" Mrs. Davies asked. "You know, of course, that my sister is dead."

"Yes, I do know that. I've been living with my aunt in Philadelphia and only returned to Baltimore recently. Last week when I heard of Flora's death, I was shocked and grieved. Flora and I were the greatest of friends."

"Really? Flora was painfully shy as a young girl. I didn't realize that she had any close friends from school. I don't remember that she ever mentioned you. How, specifically, did you happen to know her?"

What little success Hannah had had on the stage was due to always having studied her parts carefully. "We were both in Miss Selden's speech and deportment class. Flora was shy, but so was I. Perhaps in each other we recognized kindred spirits. From the moment I heard of her passing, I haven't been able to stop thinking of her."

"Nor have I," Mrs. Davies voice thickened with grief. Turning her back to Hannah, she roughly parted the curtains. As they scraped on their wooden rod, a strong beam of afternoon sunshine shot into the room.

Mrs. Davies faced her. "What is it you want? If you're here looking for a keepsake, I must warn you that I gave most of my sister's trinkets away."

"Oh, I'm not here for any such reason." Hannah drew a handkerchief out of her pocket and dabbed at the tear she'd managed to squeeze out of her eyes. The tear felt genuine enough, for despite Mrs. Davies gruff manner, Hannah sensed her grief. Her ability to empathize had been another of her strong suits as an actress. She liked the feeling of climbing into another's skin. Perhaps that was because being herself had never seemed to be much of an advantage.

"I thought that if you might tell me a bit about her last days, I could better deal with my sorrow."

"I know very little about my sister's last days," Mrs. Davies said bitterly, "save that they were unhappy. You've wasted your time."

"Who was her doctor, can you tell me that? Since I'm new to town, I'm looking for a doctor myself and I'd appreciate a recommendation."

"Doctor LeSane is the best woman's doctor in Baltimore. Now, I really must go."

Hannah had hoped to learn something more about how and why Flora Penrose had died. Visiting Flora's sister had been chancy, but Hannah had thought it was worth a try. As she swallowed her disappointment, she took in Aurelia Burnside Davies' simple furniture and plain woolen carpet. The room was as spare as Hannah's rented bedchamber.

Hannah stopped short. A portrait of Flora Penrose hung above the mantel. It was essentially the same painting Hannah had seen in Penrose's studio, and obviously done by the same hand. She would have known that even if Penrose hadn't signed it. The subject's pose and expression were identical. But in this painting of his wife Flora Penrose wore a gray silk gown. She also had, indisputably, a fine rounded bosom and womanly hips.

CHAPTER TWENTY

The Peabody Institute, the only music school in Baltimore, brought to Oliver's mind stereoscope pictures he'd seen of Paris. Inside the handsome gray stone building, he paused to admire a cast-iron staircase spiraling upward. To its left there was a reception desk.

"I'm looking for a Negro violin student named Charles Douglas," Oliver told the elderly, white-haired man seated there.

"You won't find him here. Negroes aren't allowed in this building. Not as students, not officially."

"What about unofficially?" Oliver dropped a silver dollar on the desk.

The man flipped it into his pocket and muttered, "A lot of the teachers here are Eyetalian. Some of them take on Negroes as private students. You might try Professor Credini. He's the violin maestro."

Heat shimmered off the peaked roof of a narrow row house in Fells Point and beat upon the cramped brick sidewalk within three feet of its open windows. Violin music poured through them. Oliver paused in the shade of a spindly sycamore to listen and found himself thinking of Chloe. She had had another bad night with the asthma. But it had been Mrs. Milawney she'd called for, not him. Perhaps that was better than if the child had called for her dead mother.

He told himself that he must think of some new device for gaining Chloe's confidence. Since their excursion to the Singleton mansion she had seemed a little less alarmed by him. But he was still a stranger to her. This investigation was taking too much time and energy.

Give me a straightforward robbery or shooting any day, he thought. Probing at the obscurities surrounding this train sabotage was like being sucked into quicksand. Clearly, a number of people had motive to dislike Enoch Rubman, Ben Magruder and Ira Nutwell. But who had disliked them enough to engineer a fiery train crash? And why?

Oliver's shoulder blades twitched. He looked about him. There was nothing to be seen save the sun blazing down on the empty street. Yet, a gunman might be hidden anywhere. Who had fired that bullet at him near the Rubman house? It had been a small, slim-built man and probably a young one judging from the way he'd galloped his horse. Did the attack have anything to do with the assailant Harry had warned him about? What if this mysterious enemy shifted his attention to Chloe?

The music stopped. Jolted from his unpleasant revery, he rapped on the door. A petite black maidservant wearing a head-cloth opened it.

"I'm here to see Maestro Credini."

"The maestro is busy with a student, sir."

She left Oliver seated on a straight chair in a hall so narrow and dark that he could barely make out the tin candle sconce on its rough plastered wall. The music on the other side of the closed door facing his chair began again and soared like a freed bird for several phrases. Then it ceased abruptly and Oliver heard excitable voices, one of which had a thick Italian accent.

A moment later the door was flung open by a small man with a luxurious head of black hair. Behind him stood a slim, attractive young Negro carrying a violin by its neck.

Oliver rose, introduced himself to Maestro Credini and turned to the Negro youth. "Are you Charles Douglas?"

"I am."

"I wonder if I might speak to you privately."

"About what?" The youth's eyes smoldered with suspicion.

"About a man you were seen associating with recently." Oliver gave a brief description.

"Why should I talk to you about my associates? What business is it of yours? What right do you have to hunt me down and interrupt my lesson?"

"I'm investigating a railroad accident. It's possible that this friend of yours may know something about it."

"Excuse me, excuse me, I must see to a matter of importance in, in the kitchen," the maestro stammered nervously. As he scurried past, Oliver stepped forward and shut the parlor door behind him.

He had assumed that he would be alone with the haughty black violinist, but he was mistaken. A man seated in the corner of the tiny, sparsely furnished parlor, rose and strode into the light.

He was a tall, light-skinned Negro and, in defiance of the heat, formally dressed in black broadcloth. With his regal bearing, piercing black eyes behind gold-rimmed pince-nez and handsome mane of thick gray hair, he was an impressive figure. As his sonorous voice rolled out, Oliver realized this must be Charles Douglas's grandfather, the great Frederick Douglas.

"State your business with my grandson, sir. Precisely, what is it you desire of him?"

As Oliver explained, Charles began packing his instrument into its case. "I'm not talking to this spy about my friends," he interrupted. "He's just another white man spoiling to make trouble."

The older Douglas raised an imperious hand. "Just a moment, Charlie. Don't be so hasty, nor so impolite. I will not tolerate rudeness in any member of my family. Let us hear him out."

"Sir," Oliver said, "I'm not here to make trouble. You have no idea what an honor it is for me to meet you. Before the war, my parents worked with you for the noble cause of abolition. They were Rosemary and Tucker Redcastle."

Rosemary and Tucker," Douglas repeated slowly. "You're their son? I'd heard the entire family was killed in Quantrill's raid on Lawrence."

"Quantrill butchered my parents and my brothers, but I'd already joined up with McClellan, so I escaped."

Douglas removed the pince-nez from his nose and pressed a snowy handkerchief to his eyes. "I wept when I heard of their deaths. They were fine people. I know for a fact that your mother gave up family and fortune because she had a conscience and loved your father."

"They admired you greatly."

For several long seconds, they stood in the stuffy little room regarding each other silently. It almost seemed to Oliver that the ghosts of his family were in the tiny parlor with them.

Charles Douglas appeared to feel the change in the room's atmosphere, too. He stopped fussing at his violin case. Curiously, he looked from his grandfather to Oliver.

"Charlie," Frederick Douglas said, "tell this man what he wants to know."

"Hip complaints are very common in women of your age, Mrs. Witherspoon."

Hannah gazed at Dr. LeSane through her pinz-nez. Beneath the gray wig she wore, her scalp itched. "Is there anything you can give me that will help?" she asked in her stiffest Boston accent. As she spoke, she crossed her fingers. If everything went as planned, the boy she'd hired to create a diversion in the hall should be setting off his smoke bomb about now.

Doctor LeSane consulted a thick black tome. "I can make you up a mixture of iodine and phosphate of lime combined with tannin. It's to be injected twice a day. I'll mix it up now and show you how to administer it."

Hannah wondered if presenting herself to Doctor LeSane in the guise of an old woman with hip problems had been such a good idea.

"Doctor, Doctor," LeSane's assistant cried, rushing into the examining room. "There has been some dreadful accident in the building. The hall is filled with black smoke!"

With a mild curse, LeSane rushed out the door. The moment he was gone, Hannah sprang off her chair and ran for the oak file cabinet. Fortunately Lesane was a meticulous in his file-keeping as he was in his physical examinations. Hannah found Flora Penrose's medical record almost immediately. She was tucking it into her carpetbag when she noticed another file sticking up as if it had been put away recently and in haste. The name on it caught her eye. She tucked that file into her carpetbag as well.

CHAPTER TWENTY-ONE

Gaslight twinkled in every window of Kitty Putnam's house. Sharp bursts of female laughter punctuated jovial male voices. A piano struck up "Sweet Violets."

A tall young Negro with shoulders that almost spanned the width of the entry opened the door after Oliver knocked. He appeared quite capable of tossing rowdy customers out on their ears when the occasion arose.

"Welcome sir," the Negro said politely. "Let me take your hat and conduct you to Mrs. Putnam' office."

"Certainly." Oliver followed the man down the hall.

As he waited in Mrs. Putnam's office, he heard a familiar voice outside. Curious, he opened the door and peered through. He could just see the small landing that led to the kitchen downstairs. The blue-eyed maid he'd seen on the street stood with her arms around Danny Coy. "Maureen," he was whispering in her pretty ear, "oh my Maureen. Just a few more days and I promise I'll take ye back to Dublin wearing silks and satins. I give ye my word, luv."

Coy looked up and saw Oliver. Scowling, he shooed the girl down the stairs and strode out into the light. "What are you gawkin' and eavesdroppin' at?"

"At you? Is that the girl you rescued from McKelvey? I don't blame you for taking the risk. She's lovely."

"That she is, and she's daecent, too. Just because she's workin' in a hoor house, don't get to thinkin' you can put 'yer filthy hands on her. She's doing honest work, cleanin' and cookin' and such. Try makin' up to her and the drubbin' I gave you last time will be nothin' to what I'll do to you. Get my meanin'?"

"It's crystal clear. I wouldn't dream of interfering with-- Maureen is it?"

"That's her name, and she's as innocent as the angels and twice as good."

"Pretty little thing that she is, you'd better get her out of here or she won't stay innocent."

Coy's face darkened. "I'm doing me best, man. Maureen won't be serving hoors and washing their dirty sheets much longer if I have anything to say about it."

Would he have anything to say about it, Oliver wondered. What did a street tough like Coy have to offer a beauty like Maureen?

Coy hurried away just as Kitty Putnam came around the corner. "Mr. Redcastle, I'm delighted. Have you come on business or pleasure this time?"

"The former, I'm afraid. I'm here to meet an old friend named Jake Jaggard."

Kitty's eyes lit with amusement. "If Jake Jaggard is your friend, then you've no business being a stranger to pleasure. Jake's been a frequent visitor here these last few days, very frequent."

"I can imagine."

Jake Jaggard's reputation with the ladies was legendary. Oliver hadn't been surprised when Charles Douglas, at his grandfather's insistence, had set up this rendezvous with Jake. Doubtless Jake had thought it would be a good joke to meet in a whorehouse.

Kitty took Oliver's arm and led him across the hall. The parlor was floridly furnished in red velvet and gilt and crowded with men, most here for the encampment. Several danced with gaudily dressed women. Under their paint, the girls looked young. Many appeared to be Irish colleens fresh off the boat.

Oliver spotted Jaggard lounging on a loveseat with a lush mulatto woman on his lap and two bosomy young blondes draped to either side. His eyes, beneath straight black brows, danced.

Lifting his champagne glass, he called out, "Why, if it isn't Preacher Redcastle come to pay his respects. New friends are silver, but old adversaries are fool's gold. Becky, Sal, Therese, this is Oliver Redcastle, detective extraordinaire, a lawman with more derring-do in his trigger finger than Robin Hood and Sherlock Holmes combined. Olly, meet the ladies. A more accommodating bevy of beauties you're unlikely to discover. Say the word and they'll put a smile on that dour mug of yours."

"Not tonight."

With a mock sigh, Jaggard uncoiled his arms from around the blondes' waists and shooed the other girl off his lap. "You always were a spoilsport. What can I do for you?"

"You can put on your hat and come outside. We need to talk."

"I knew you were here to ruin my party."

A half an hour later, the two men's heels clicked on the cobblestones paving Thames Street at the foot of Broadway. A clock struck midnight. Fog rolled in off the harbor, wreathing the masts of the clippers, schooners, bugeyes and China traders jostling each other in the rising tide along the Fells Point waterfront. The fog added a salty tang to air already flavored by overripe privies well steamed on the blistering anvil of the day's heat.

Under Jaggard's tall hat, his hair was now neatly brushed. Gloves that matched his skirted jacket and pale gray pantaloons encased his hands, and he carried a silver-headed cane. Across his embroidered vest he sported his trademark diamond-studded watch. Despite his height, his movements were elegant and compact. Gentleman Jake counted among his many other accomplishments, a talent for cat burglary.

"This is a rough part of town," Oliver said. "Is it wise to flash that blinder?"

Jaggard smiled lazily and rubbed an affectionate thumb over the huge gem glittering on his waistcoat. "Worried about my security? I'm touched, but I do believe I can take care of myself."

Oliver shrugged. In the annals of the Pinkertons, Gentleman Jake Jaggard had to be the cleverest and most effective criminal on record. Allan Pinkerton had once estimated that in his twenty years of lawbreaking Jaggard had stolen over four million dollars without once resorting to bloodshed--and without ever getting caught. He had robbed his millions from international banking firms, European businesses and jewelry firms. When not thieving he lived like a lord in London or Paris and consorted with nobility who treated him like a long lost brother. Now here he was in Baltimore, big as life and twice as jaunty. "I'm damned curious to know why you're here, Jake?"

Jaggard smiled his maddening smile. "Why, I'm here for the encampment, what else? I fought for the Union, after all. Why should it surprise you that I'm here to meet with some of my old comrades in arms?"

"Do they know that when the Confederates offered to pay deserters with rifles $30, you slipped through McClellan's lines, collected the money and then came back through West Virginia?"

Jaggard widened his eyes. "Did I really do that, Ollie? Thirty pieces of silver? My, what an enterprising fellow I was, even in my misspent youth. But then I was always ambitious to lead a life writ large."

"Writ large with larceny."

"I suppose so, but you would see it in that light, wouldn't you Ollie? You always were a bit of a puritan. You even dress like one. Look at that black coat you're wearing. You could stand up and preach a sermon in it." Jaggard's teasing voice took on a harder timber. "What is this about? Why have you been bothering poor young Charles Douglas over his--quite innocent, I assure you--acquaintance with me? He knows me because I served with his father and looked him up for old times sake."

Tersely, Oliver explained himself. Jaggard shook his handsome head and then pointed where tavern lights glowed in the thickening fog "There's a sailor's dive called The Cat's Eye down there. Let's see if we can find ourselves a berth."

In his fancy clothes, Gentleman Jake Jaggard looked as out of place in The Cat's Eye as an orchid in a cabbage patch. Ignoring the curious stares of the other patrons, Jaggard cut a straight path through the heat, body odors and greasy smoke to an empty table at the rear of the establishment.

Oliver caught sight of John L. Sullivan at the bar. In deference to the heat, the boxer wore shirtsleeves and suspenders. The flush on his cheeks and bull neck suggested he'd spent the evening swaggering from tavern to tavern. While a group of chums, including Danny Coy, cheered him on, he poured a full tankard down his throat. Oliver walked over, thanked him for his help during the brawl at Kernan's and shook his hand. Sullivan merely bellowed a laugh and delivered a slap to his back. As he staggered from the friendly but stinging blow, he noticed Coy regarding him as a snake might an unwary prairie dog.

When Oliver sat down at the back of the tavern, Jaggard drawled, "Wasn't that John L. Sullivan, the boxer? When did you and he become amigos?"

"Last night he helped me out of a bad situation. He only did it because he enjoys a fight. Just now when he slapped me on the back I felt as if I'd been hit with a sledgehammer. I wouldn't want to be on his wrong side."

"You wouldn't want to be on my wrong side, either. Yet you're accusing me of sabotaging trains. Why should you think I have any connection with this B&O mishap?"

"You were overheard saying that Ira Nutwell, one of the men killed in the accident, deserved to burn in hell."

Jaggard raised an eyebrow. "Might I inquire as to the identity of your informant?"

"So, it's true. You did know and hate Nutwell."

"I did. If I'd known he was on that train, I might have incinerated him myself. The villain deserved a fiery fate. But I didn't know. In fact, I didn't arrive in this country until several days after the accident, and I have a passport stamp to prove it."

"What was your connection with Nutwell? Why do you hate him so much?"

"Hate is a word I reserve for worthy enemies. Perhaps despise and abominate are closer to the mark. I served under Nutwell in a little known and unrecorded action which took place late in the war. A company of Rebs were dug in on a hill in West Virginia. Their sharpshooters were picking our men off like clay pigeons.

"Nutwell got the bright idea of tunneling into the hill and threw a company of escaped Negroe slaves into the task. The Rebs heard them digging and did some digging of their own. They sunk a shaft, filled it with gunpowder and set it off. The center of the hill caved in and all the men tunneling inside were buried alive. That's the kind of commanding officer Ira Nutwell was."

"The Negroes who died must have had friends and relatives. They'd have good reason to hold a grudge against Nutwell. Why did you go to the trouble of looking up Charles Douglas when you got into town? Does he have any connection with this tunnel business?"

Jaggard's laugh rang out. "You think Charlie might have blown Nutwell and his pals to smithereens? Redcastle, the day will come when your suspicious nature will keep your nose pressed to the wrong side of the pearly gates. I looked up Charlie because I knew and liked his father, and I'm an admirer of his grandfather's. Good Lord, man, Charlie is a youngster. His sole ambition in life is to play the violin in a concert hall."

"Do you think he's likely to realize that ambition?" Oliver asked curiously.

"Alas, I fear white audiences will never support a black performer who isn't giving a minstrel show. But you've got to admire the Douglases. I appreciate any man with the guts to reach for the golden apple, whether it tumbles to him or not."

Through the tavern's smoky atmosphere, Oliver gazed at

Gentleman Jake thoughtfully. If anybody had reached for golden apples, it was he. What's more, he'd plucked quite a few that were forbidden fruit.

Jaggard declared after he drained the rest of his glass, "Neither Charlie nor I had anything to do with this railroad mishap. Doubtless, that's exactly what it was, an accident. Which is good news for all of us, for it may mean there's a God in heaven who metes out justice."

A quarter of an hour later Oliver and Jaggard were outside again. The cobblestones still steamed from the day's heat, and the fog had thickened. Oliver said, "I'm not swallowing your story that you've crossed the ocean for this encampment and for no other reason. Sure you're not planning to rob a bank? I wouldn't put it past you."

Jaggard rapped the point of his cane on a hitching post and chuckled. "Why should you care? I hear you've quit the Pinkertons."

"True."

"So, there's no call for us to be enemies. Actually, Redcastle, I've always admired you. You've got grit. I admire that in a man, even a sworn enemy. Truthfully, I'm relieved that we're no longer at odds. In fact, I'm prepared to make you an offer. If you should need help solving this railroad matter, my services are available--as long as I remain a guest in the city, that is."

"How long will that be?"

"I'm registered at Barnums through the 23rd. After that. . ." Jaggard broke off as the clatter of pounding feet broke into the stillness.

"Get him, boys! Twist his damned balls off!"

Oliver whirled around in time to see McKelvy and his toughs materialize from the fog like imps from hell.

CHAPTER TWENTY-TWO

McKelvy's hooligans carried knives, saps, hammers, hay hooks and fish spikes. One pug twirled a two-inch thick rope with a knot at the end the size of a man's head.

Oliver dodged it, but a split second later a pair of brass knuckles connected with the back of his neck. He reeled into a piling.

Rolling to his left, he narrowly avoided tumbling into the filthy water slopping against the rotted pilings. As he scrambled to his feet, he saw Jaggard stab one of the yeggs with his cane, which had now been transformed into a sword stick. The hoodlum, a piggish tough with a keloid scar that ran the length of his right cheek, staggered back clutching his side. Blood stained his shirt.

Jaggard's sword stick flashed and flickered in the gaslight. The fallen hooligan's companion backed off.

McKelvy danced around Jaggard screaming, "Ye lily livers! It's only two against the seven of us!" He raised his club to bring it down on Oliver.

His own cane had jammed into a crack in the rough wood wharf. He tried to pull it loose, but it wouldn't budge. Eluding McKelvy's wild swings, he kicked one of the other charging thugs and sent him reeling off the dock into the water. Distracted by his cohort's thrashing and screaming, McKelvy looked away from Oliver who tried again to dislodge his cane.

Jaggard, seemingly untroubled by being hopelessly outnumbered, sliced and twirled his deadly swordstick. He'd just managed to draw blood from another of McKelvy's following when Oliver finally freed his cane. He discharged its single shot at McKelvy. The report echoed on the slick cobblestones as the bullet struck the bully in the shoulder. He reeled backward.

"I'll bash yer brains in for that! I'll make bloody sawdust out of ye'!" Ignoring his wound, he twirled his club over his head as if it were a battleaxe. Oliver jammed the cane between McKelvy's legs. It caught him between the knees and he tumbled chin first onto the slick cobblestones.

Behind the veils of fog muffling the streetlamp, a deep voice shouted a coarse oath. John L. Sullivan emerged from the mist.

"What have we here?" he cried as he took in the situation. "Five against two? If there's anything I can't stomach, it's an unfair fight!" And with that, he cocked his famous fists and waded in. Danny Coy and the other drinkers in his party yelped with glee and followed suit.

McKelvy's gang saw their disadvantage. Abandoning their weapons and dragging their wounded leader with them, they fled into the night. When nothing remained of them but the tattoo of their retreating feet, Sullivan turned to Oliver. Winded and bloody, he had sagged onto one of the pilings that lined the wharf.

"Here and I thought I was leadin' a stimulatin' life," Sullivan chortled, "but judging from our few run-ins, you outshine me by far."

"Thanks for your help." Oliver smiled ruefully. "That's twice you've rescued me. If you ever need a favor, I owe you."

"Oh, 'twas nothing, lad, nothing at all. Me and me pals needed some exercise. We'd been on our arses too long in that filthy bar. Besides, it looks to me as if you already had some pretty handy help." He pointed at Gentleman Jake who was trying to fish his silk hat out of the water where it had been knocked during the fray. The wounded thug who'd fallen in had long since disappeared from view. Either he'd paddled to safety someplace else or he was on the bottom.

"It's no use, Jake!" Oliver shouted. "That water contains more foul matter than a ragman's chamberpot. You won't want to have that hat on your head again."

"I suppose you're right." Jaggard sighed. "That particular chapeau cost the earth. I shall have a hellish time finding one to equal it in Baltimore. Who were those excessively bellicose riff-raff, by the way?"

"Just some waterfront thugs I met in an unfortunate situation a couple of nights ago." Oliver shot Danny Coy a meaningful glance. Coy, who sat on a curb using his shirtsleeve to clean blood off his brass knuckles, looked innocent. "I hardly know them."

"Nevertheless, you must have made quite an impression. They certainly seem to know you."

"And now they know me," Sullivan said with a satisfied guffaw. Playfully, he danced about the cobbles, shadow boxing the wraiths of mist coiling in off the water. Despite his large size, he stepped and wove as nimbly as a ballet dancer.

Jaggard and Oliver exchanged a few more words with Sullivan, and each shook the fighter's big hand. They watched as he and his cronies retreated down the street singing snatches of bawdy songs.

A hack rounded the corner and Jaggard signaled it. Inside, he said, "Well, that was amusing."

Oliver dabbed a handkerchief against a throbbing spot at the back of his neck. "I'm glad you're amused. I can't say the same for myself. You realize that fellow who fell into the water never got out?"

"Then we've diminished the population of waterfront rats. The town fathers should thank us."

"Of course you'd see it that way."

"What's happened? Your conscience getting to you? I'm right in thinking you were raised Quaker, aren't I?"

Oliver nodded. "My father never read anything but the Bible. He was something close to a saint."

"Sounds like a damned bore to me. You must have thought

so, too, because you certainly haven't taken him as your model. What was he like when he wasn't reading the Bible?"

"A pathetic failure as a farmer. Once my mother was driven to making coffee out of grated dried carrots when we had unexpected company. What about you? Were you born without a conscience or did you just shuck it off somewhere along the way?"

"Come on, Ollie. If you go poking your nose into dung heaps, you're bound to dislodge a beetle or two. The best thing to do with a beetle is step on it before it dirties your gaiters."

"Jake, I didn't come to Baltimore looking for trouble."

"You go everywhere looking for trouble. It's your nature. You're not so different from your preacher father, after all. You've got the soul of a reformer."

Oliver admitted, "Since taking on this damned railroad investigation, I've stepped into one bear trap after another. When I moved to this city, nobody knew who I was. I felt I had a good chance of starting fresh. Now I've got enemies swarming out of every corner like a damned pack of fire ants. And in most cases I don't even know why."

Jaggard clucked unsympathetically. "You take these things too seriously. I promise you, a dispassionate view of events makes them easier to accept. After a night like this, you should reward yourself with a day of rest and refreshment. Sweet air to clear your lungs, sunshine to warm your skin and beautiful women to delight your eyes--that's what a man needs. Did you know that Sarah Bernhardt and Oscar Wilde are both in town?"

Oliver leaned his weary head against the hack's frame. His braincase throbbed like a gypsy violin. "This Wilde fellow is a poet, isn't he?"

"A poet and playwright. He's here lecturing on art for art's sake. In love with himself, of course, but quite the rapier wit. You might find him amusing."

"Right now it will take more than a stuck-on-himself Brit to amuse me. I took my daughter to see Bernhardt perform the other night. Chloe's only seven, but she was thrilled."

"As it happens, Wilde and the divine Sarah and I are old chums. I'll be escorting the pair of them on a carriage ride in the park tomorrow morning. Bring your little girl and I'll make sure she meets Sarah. Chance of a lifetime, Redcastle. Bernhardt is one for the history books. Wilde, too, if I'm any judge. A man with a tongue as sharp as his is bound to make his mark."

The next morning Mrs. Milawney dressed Chloe in pink muslin trimmed with narrow velvet and rosettes of silk. When she joined Oliver in the front hall, he exclaimed, "You look like the prettiest flower in the rose garden!"

Chloe eyed him curiously. He guessed she must wonder how he'd acquired the bruises decorating his face but was too shy to ask. She said, "Are we really going to meet Sarah Bernhardt?"

"We'll try our best."

They caught the Madison Avenue streetcar to Druid Hill Park where they hired a horse-drawn phaeton to take them around the lake drive. It was a beautiful high summer day. The sun, a fiery ball in a sky of cloudless blue, promised to make the afternoon another scorcher. But it had not yet burnt the morning dew off the turf bordering the lake. The odors of new cut grass and leafy trees at the height of their summer splendor infused the air.

At this hour the lake drive at Druid Hill Park was clearly a place to see and be seen. Even little Chloe seemed to realize that. Her eyes were bright as she looked around, taking in the hacks, pole chairs and bicyclists, the trotting thoroughbreds with their jingling harness.

"Oh, there's Sarah Bernhardt!" she cried.

Sure enough, ensconced in an elegant brougham opposite Jake Jaggard and another man who must be Oscar Wilde, was the famed French actress. Jaggard tipped his top hat. A moment later his driver had stopped his equipage on the grass at the side of the road. Oliver pulled his rental phaeton alongside.

After Jake made the introductions, he said, "So, Redcastle, this is your little girl? She's much prettier than you deserve!"

Jaggard jumped down lightly, crossed to Chloe and kissed her hand. Blushing, the child stared at him with open admiration. Indeed, he was a sight to behold in his morning coat, striped trousers and silk cravat. The pearl-colored hat he wore was a more than adequate replacement for the one lost at Fells Point.

Oliver looked at Jaggard's companions. Oscar Wilde was a fleshy young man with a florid Irish face, humorous eyes and what looked to be a perpetual sneer on his full lips. In contrast, Sarah Bernhardt was a slender, aristocratic looking woman in her late thirties. Elegantly dressed in pale green silk, she wore a hat of white straw trimmed with green velvet and crystal beads. The woman definitely had an air about her. Yet the magnetism she projected in the daylight hours didn't begin to equal the impact of her stage presence.

"Bring the oh-so-charming child to me," Bernhardt demanded. If her handsome papa agrees, we shall take her with us for a ride about the lake." She tapped Wilde's knee with her fan. "What do you say, cherie?"

"Oh, by all means," Wilde agreed, "make the child our companion. The only danger is that I may swoon, surrounded by such youth and beauty. It's a risk, but I'm ready to make the sacrifice."

"You tease me," Bernhardt said and smacked his plump knuckles with the tip of her parasol.

Seeing the delight on Chloe's small face, Oliver gave his consent and agreed to wait by the lake until they should return in about an hour. After delivering his rental phaeton over to an attendant, he walked to Druid Lake's grassy verge and surveyed the scene.

It seemed as if half of Baltimore was taking advantage of the fine summer morning. Children flew kites and sailed toy boats on strings. Family groups and couples, some with picnic hampers already open, lounged on blankets. An artist had even set up an easel. He was painting a young woman. A parasol shaded her face, but her robe of white percale clung fetchingly to her slender figure.

Oliver took a hard second look and realized that the young woman was Mrs. Hannah Kinchman. No wonder he'd failed to recognize her at first glance. Her dress and demeanor were entirely different from what he'd seen of her before. She looked light as thistledown in her summer gown--a flirtatious belle gilded with sunlight. At that instant the breeze carried her laughter to Oliver's ears. The woman was a witch, a veritable shapeshifter.

The artist painting her was a slender man with a head of showy black curls and a way of striking a pose that brought to mind a bigamist safecracker Oliver had known in Argentina. This fellow playing Pygmalion to Hannah Kinchman's Aphrodite must be Beacher Penrose.

"Why are you ogling that pretty young woman? If you want to detach her from Beacher, I suggest you go about it more subtly."

Oliver whirled. "Laura!"

The vision Laura Singleton presented drove Hannah Kinchman from his head. In her perky straw hat, she was the incarnation of spring. Golden curls framed her lovely face. Her sea green eyes made him think of wood nymphs.

"What are you doing here?" they each exclaimed in unison. Both laughed.

He explained that he had brought Chloe to meet Sarah Bernhardt and Oscar Wilde. "Is Griff here with you?"

A shadow crossed Laura's face. She stared out at the lake. "I came here with friends." She pointed at a pair of couples lounging on the grass about fifty yards away.

"Ollie, I don't think you understand how it is with Griff and me. You think of Griff the way he was when we were children--always so gay. The war changed him. He rarely leaves the house. Most of the time he sleeps, or sits in the garden and broods. He has what they call the melancholia. I try to be a good wife, but there are days when I just have to get away. This was one of them."

He said, "The war affected a lot of men in strange ways. I

know of fellows who went home to their families and took to living in the attics like ghosts."

"I'm married to a fellow like that, Olly. Oh, he's not like the poor maimed hulks begging handouts at train stations. When we have visitors, he talks to them. He reads the paper. He even writes letters. But he's not the man I fell in love with."

"Griff may recover."

"He'll never recover. Do you remember how handsome he was, how charming?"

Oliver nodded. He'd both worshipped and envied Griff. There had been moments, in his jealous infatuation with Laura, that he'd even hated his cousin. Now those moments filled him with guilt.

Laura sighed. "The life I pictured was so different than the one we have." A faint blush stained her cheek. "I thought we would have children, such beautiful children--four of them, two perfect boys and two perfect girls. I was a silly fool."

"Isn't it possible. . .Could you and Griff. . ."

"Have children?" Laura shook her head. "That's not going to happen, either. Soon, it will be too late for me to even think of it. Oh Ollie, I did so want my own family!" She pressed a small hand against her breast. "Just acknowledging it to you like this hurts me."

His hand went out and she grasped it, never breaking eye contact. He took a step toward her. The crack of a rifle rang out and his knees buckled.

CHAPTER TWENTY-THREE

Marshal Rackley pressed a fat thumb to the plaster bandaging Oliver's wounded neck. His rude guffaw rattled. "I hope this little nick won't affect your aim when you take on our man, Gloger."

Oliver shook the smirking Rackley off, unamused. Had the bullet he'd taken in the park hit an inch to the left, it would have got him in the spine or pierced an artery. He was damn lucky it hadn't done any serious damage.

He eyed the chief's bulging stomach, stuffed with the gargantuan buffet breakfast of sausage, bacon and eggs he'd just wolfed down. It had been served on silver platters by a silent black man wearing a starched white jacket. The Negro was now discreetly clearing away the litter of soiled plates and cutlery.

Rackley said, "You're lucky that slug didn't nip you in the windpipe. You wouldn't be standing here telling the tale."

"I wish I had more of a tale to tell. The fellow who shot me got clean away. I don't even have a description of him."

Rackley hoisted a champagne bottle out of a silver ice bucket. After popping the cork against the lodge's beamed ceiling, he topped up his half empty juice glass. When he offered the bottle, Oliver shook his head. "I need to keep my wits about me."

Before dawn he'd driven a rented light wagon to The Reeds, a private hunting lodge in a remote spot north and east of the city. Situated on a marshy spit of land jutting into the Chesapeake, the lodge had been furnished with self-conscious rusticity and decorated with an assortment of weapons, carved decoys and stuffed animal heads. The place was an ideal spot for duck hunting, serious drinking and secret meetings.

"Hot one today," Edson Bailey remarked. He refilled his juice glass with champagne. As he hoisted it to his mouth, several drops splashed onto his swelling shirtfront. Despite the hazy dawn light promising another hot day, he wore a Norfolk jacket over checkered pants tucked loosely into Wellington boots. The other two men in the room, Clarence Sanders and Samuel Gloger, were in shirtsleeves and suspenders. This was Oliver's first glimpse of the man whose marksmanship Rackley had so often touted.

Gloger was slightly built and sickly looking. His prominent Adam's apple bobbed every time he swallowed and his watery blue eyes hid like furtive fish behind his droopy lids. Despite his forgettable looks he had an air of confidence. He, too, was drinking his juice straight.

Though Oliver had been introduced to Gloger when he'd arrived at the lodge, the two had stayed on opposite sides of the great room. Like gladiators who knew they would be drawing each other's blood on the field of battle, they both wanted to keep their relationship impersonal while they sized each other up.

Several times that morning Oliver had caught Gloger's calculating glance assessing him. Now the sharpshooter crossed the room and said, "Rackley tells me that you're a right decent shot, and that I'll have my work cut out to outbang you this morning."

Oliver shrugged. "I used to be pretty good. Lately, I've been too busy to keep in practice." That was at least partly true. He hadn't taken out the Remington-Beals since killing Flatt.

Gloger's pale eyes gleamed. He drained his juice and set his glass down on an elephant foot table where it was immediately swept up by the servant. "A man needs to practice his skill or it goes south. Me, I fire my guns just about every day. Lucky for me, what I shoot at don't usually shoot back. Rackley tells me you've been dodging bullets ever since you come to Baltimore. Got any idea who's after you?"

"None." After he'd been nicked at Druid Hill Park, he'd pressed his handkerchief to the wound and chased through the crowd of picnickers. None of the shocked onlookers he'd questioned had been able to point him at the shooter who'd melted into the trees unnoticed. Finally, Laura had insisted he see a doctor.

Now, as he looked into Gloger's cold eyes, it occurred to him that he might have been the shooter. But so far as he knew, Gloger had no reason to want to kill him. Besides, if the man was as good with a gun as they claimed, he wouldn't have missed his mark.

He seemed to read Oliver's mind. "You're lucky. The fellow after you ain't much of a marksman. Still, I'd watch myself real close if I were you. Luck has a way of skipping out on a man just when he needs it most."

"That's why it's best not to need it," Rackley said, coming up and giving Gloger a bone-jarring slap on the back. "Now here's a fellow who doesn't need to depend on luck. See that handsome object on the wall in back of you?" Rackley pointed at an elaborate trophy topped by an eagle perched on a wreath balanced over an embroidered banner. The banner was decorated by a necklace of wreaths from which was suspended a gold and silver arrow.

"That's the Palma," Rackley declared. "Our Gloger here won it at Creedmore. That's the most prestigious shooting competition there is, you know."

Oliver made admiring noises. Actually, he recognized the trophy, which was a replica of a Roman legionary standard commissioned from Tiffany. He had one like it stuck away in a trunk somewhere in his aunt's attic.

Rackley gave Oliver a challenging look. "Well, Redcastle, what do you think of our little business proposition?"

"Sounds interesting." And it did. During breakfast, Rackley, Bailey and Sanders had described a dredging operation they were putting together with two other silent partners, both of whom wished to remain anonymous. One, a highly placed official in Washington, had alerted the men to a government bonanza in the form of a Rivers and Harbors bill. When the bill was passed, as it soon would be, investors in their newly formed dredging company stood to make fortunes.

"It's the chance of a lifetime," Rackley said. "If you want in, put your money where your mouth is and soon. We'll get those government contracts if we're Johnny-on-the-spot. Everyone you see here is fully invested and we're making our move. The equipment was a little more expensive than we anticipated, so we're prepared to take one more partner. What do you say?"

"I'll need to give it some thought."

"Don't make the mistake of fiddling when Rome burns. We need all our ducks in a row. Either fish or cut bait. What's it to be?"

Oliver managed to keep from smiling at Rackley's mixed metaphors. "It's a lot of money. I need a few days."

The marshal held up his right hand and wiggled two fingers. Two, that's all we can give you, two days. After that, we'll look elsewhere. With a deal like this one, we won't have trouble finding an investor with some guts. Now, what about showing us some of your fancy shooting?"

A quarter of an hour later Rackley, Bailey, Sanders, Gloger and Oliver stood outside the lodge. The sun had just burned the morning mist off the marsh grass. A breeze lifted the fronds on a pair of willows trailing their leaves at the water's edge, some five-hundred yards to the right. Parallel to the water, Rackley and Bailey had set up a series of rectangular targets situated at ranges of 200, 400, 500 and 600 yards.

"Same rules as Creedmoor," Rackley announced as he came back through the tall grass. "Your firearms should weigh less than ten pounds with a minimum trigger pull of three. No telescopic sights or set triggers.

Oliver handed over his Remington-Beals for inspection.

"Not many of those around," Gloger said as he took his British Whitworth out of its tooled leather case.

Oliver nodded. His rifle was one of only 800 manufactured in 1867. He'd acquired it in a card game and never found a weapon he liked better for accuracy.

"How many men have you shot dead?"

"No way of knowing. During the war I fired at a lot of Reb officers and saw them fall. For all I know, most lived to tell the tale." This was not actually true, but why brag about spilling blood in that bloody war.

"The Federals I hit never took their faces out of the dirt," Gloger declared with an air of satisfaction. "I always made sure they did the flippety flop before I turned my attention elsewhere. There's only one Federal I know for sure I didn't kill, and I left him on purpose."

"How was that?"

As Gloger studied Oliver's face, a sly grin tugged at his thin lips. "It was during a skirmish down in West Virginia. I was walking through the woods, separated from my company, when I come upon a Union soldier. Big handsome fella' from Maine. He was gut shot and suffering something terrible. Poor s.o.b. was trying to hold his insides in with his hands while flies squirmed all over him so thick they looked like a living carpet. It was a pitiful sight. He begged me to shoot him in the head so he'd die quick. I wouldn't do it. When I went back next day to check on him, he'd cut his own throat. I still chuckle when I think about that."

Oliver felt his gorge rising. He also felt Gloger watching him closely. Was the man trying to rattle him?

"You know," Gloger said, "I think I might know who you really are, Redcastle. When you were shooting for the Federals, did you used to wear a little red feather in your hat?"

"Now and again." It had been a silly affectation, a way of flaunting his deadly skill in the enemy's face. But then he'd only been sixteen at the time.

Gloger hooted. "Glory be! So I'm finally meeting up with the deadly Red Feather boy. Did you know there was a bounty on your hide? You were a regular legend around our campfires. I tried to stalk and kill you once myself. Didn't succeed, though. It was one of the big disappointments of my military career.

Five minutes later the shooting began.

CHAPTER TWENTY-FOUR

"**S**o, what happened?" Harry asked. "Did you show this Gloger fellow who was boss?"

Oliver drained his mug and then wiped beer foam from his lips. "Not at all. Gloger won."

Harry's jaw dropped. "You jest. Ollie, you're the best."

"Gloger is better. Simple as that."

In fact, the last round of the shooting competition at The Reeds had not been simple. During the first three rounds Oliver and Gloger had matched each other shot for shot. It was only after Rackley moved their targets to 600 yards that the balance shifted.

As in every round before, Oliver and Gloger had faced two parallel targets. They'd had three minutes to take their shot. When the sun rose, the wind had come up with it. It sent clouds hurrying across the pale sky, skimmed ripples over the water and ruffled the tall marsh grass. At six hundred yards, even the slightest breeze could affect a bullet's trajectory. So Oliver had kept one eye on the tall grass. In shooting matches he'd learned to take his shot during a lull in the wind. Sometimes waiting for the drop wasn't so easy, not with the pressure building inside you.

"Feeling the lump?" Gloger had whispered.

The lump, of course, was the tightness that rises in a shooter's throat when the pressure starts getting to him. When Oliver had been sixteen, he'd never felt the lump. Now, at thirty-six, his nerves felt jumpy.

"One minute gone," Rackley, the timekeeper, had called out.

"You know," Gloger had muttered, I mentioned I tried to kill Red Feather and didn't get my man. But I did shoot a man who wore a red feather in his hat. It was at Grundy Creek in '63. You remember Grundy Creek?"

Oliver had felt his chest constrict. Grundy Creek was one of his personal nightmares. He and his best friend and shooting partner, Ty Conlon, had been camped on top of a hill, waiting to pick off a party of Rebs they'd heard were raiding the area. Ty had lost his own hat the night before. The sun was high and since his fair, freckled skin burned easily, he'd borrowed Oliver's hat. Not a quarter of an hour after he put it on a bullet from an unseen sniper had caught him in the throat. Oliver had managed to slip away from the hidden Reb sniper's deadly fire with a whole skin, but he'd never again worn a red feather.

Now, in a knee-jerk reaction, he squeezed the trigger. Unluckily, the wind rose at the same instant and his slug punched into the target an inch wide of its mark. Thirty seconds later the traitor wind dropped and Gloger took his shot. It hit the bullseye.

"And you're telling me this weasel Gloger rattled you?" Harry Barnett shook his head in disgust. "You really are turning into a weak sister."

It was the day after the shooting match. Harry had surprised Oliver by appearing on his doorstep and offering to buy lunch. Over oysters and potato salad in a noisy tavern near the Market Exchange, he'd filled Harry in on the progress of his investigation for Rockefeller. In turn, Harry had described the measures the Pinkertons were taking to protect the President and his cabinet during their upcoming visit to Baltimore.

Harry leaned forward, his dark eyes glistening. "Gloger sounds like a crude piece of work. Demand a rematch."

"No, thank you." Oliver reflected that at one time he would have been furious about being outmaneuvered by a man like Gloger. He'd been so proud of his skill with a gun. Now the dead soldiers who plagued his dreams, including Conlon, made that misguided pride dust in his mouth.

Gloger had invoked the ghosts of his past and they had risen up and betrayed him. Or maybe he just hadn't cared who was the better marksman. Or maybe some instinct had warned him that it would be better to lose that match than to win it. What did it matter?

Now, he smiled wryly at Harry and changed the subject. "I need some advice. The real purpose of this shindig at The Reeds was a business deal. Tell me what you think of it." He outlined the offer he'd had from Rackley and Bailey. When he finished, Harry shook his head.

"Sounds like some D.C. swindler's palm has been greased. No doubt about it, if this Rivers and Harbors bill goes through, it'll put a lot of money into the pockets of the right people."

"The right people?"

"Don't play innocent, Ollie. You know how the honeypot gets divied up in Washington. Rackley and his pals have obviously got a line straight into the committee overseeing the bids. If they've paid off the right officials, they're sure of getting the fattest contracts. That's probably why they need more money. It's not for equipment. They need to grease more palms."

"Before he was killed, Enoch Rubman was part of this cabal."

"Think there's a connection between that and his so-called accident?"

"At this point, I don't know. But it's a possibility." Oliver thought of the two partners who hadn't been at The Reeds because they wished to remain anonymous. Who were they? "So it sounds to you as if Rackley and Company have bribed their way inside the pork barrel and are offering me a taste of the bacon fat?"

"It would if I didn't know that President Arthur has threatened to veto that Rivers and Harbors bill. If he does, there might be enough votes to override his veto. One thing I do know, I wouldn't risk my money on a chance like that. Nor do your co-conspirators in the deal sound like trustworthy characters.

They must know what a chancy thing it is now. Maybe they'd prefer to gamble your money instead of theirs."

Oliver squeezed lemon onto his last oyster. Had Rackley and his pals known about Arthur's threatened veto when they'd made their original investment, he wondered. He doubted it. But they must know now. Maybe Harry was right about the real reason they were soliciting silent partners. If Arthur's veto went through and their scheme failed, they'd have outsider money to soften the blow to their own pocketbooks. They'd decided he was the pigeon they were going to pluck.

A familiar voice cut into the tavern's noise. "Well, as I live and breathe. If it isn't my old familiars, Harry and Oliver. Now, what are you two plotting at, I wonder."

A beautifully dressed individual threaded his way delicately through the oyster shells and chicken bones littering the tavern's sawdust floor.

"Good God, it's Gentleman Jake Jaggard!" Harry exclaimed.

"None other," Gentleman Jake agreed. A hard twinkle glittered in his eyes. He stopped in front of their booth, wedged the tip of his ebony cane carefully into a small crack in the plank floor and stacked his smoothly gloved hands on the cane's gold head. "It's beginning to seem like a family reunion," he remarked. "I don't suppose you two will have the grace to invite me to share your dubious libations in this gustatory third circle of hell."

"You're welcome to sit down with us," Oliver said.

"Now that you mention it, no thank you. I happen to have business elsewhere in the neighborhood. Actually, I'm here on an errand for your delightful housekeeper, Redcastle. I must say, she does brew up an excellent cup of tea." Jake took an envelope out of his pocket and flourished it. "I stopped by your house. Naturally, I was concerned for your health after that unpleasant shooting incident in the park. Mrs. Milawney told me I'd find you here and asked me to deliver this. It's a telegram she received just after you left along with something from a lady who also stopped to inquire about your health."

"I'm touched." Oliver accepted the envelope and slipped it under his plate.

Jaggard tipped his top hat. "Now that I've seen you're in fine fettle despite the lead flying about your head, I must be off."

"Important business?" Harry Barnett inquired with false sweetness.

Jaggard showed a set of gleaming teeth. "Very. Actually, I have an appointment with a lady. Miss Sarah Bernhardt is in town and I've promised to escort her on a little shopping expedition."

"As long as you don't plan to do any shopping at the local banks," Harry retorted.

Jaggard merely laughed, tipped his hat again and sauntered out.

Oliver and Harry watched the elegant cat burglar make a graceful exit through the tavern's swinging doors.

"Why's that son-of-a-bitch here, I wonder," Harry muttered.

"Maybe it's just as he says and he's here to enjoy the reunion."

"That slick customer didn't come all the way across the Atlantic merely to slap a few backs. He's about as loyal to the American flag as the Russian Czar. Jaggard's up to something."

"Whatever he's up to, it doesn't concern me. I haven't been hired to protect a bank."

"Nor I," Harry agreed. "I have enough on my plate to see that the President doesn't catch a bullet the way Garfield did. Still, I wonder. . ." He shrugged. "Well, aren't you going to open your packet?"

Oliver slit the seal and withdrew a yellowed newspaper folded small. A note from Hannah Kinchman had been clipped to it with a pin. "My landlady, Mrs. Battaile, keeps a stack of old newspapers for her boarders to peruse in the parlor. I found this interview with your cousin and thought it might interest you. I have other information and will stop by to inquire after your health later."

Oliver glanced at the article, which was dated April 18, 1882. It was, indeed, an interview with his cousin--apparently one of a series of articles with local war heroes written as part of a buildup to the approaching encampment. In the article the reporter quoted Griff on the horrors of his experience at Point Lookout.

"What's that?" Harry asked.

"Nothing of importance. I'll look at it later." Oliver replaced it and slipped a telegram marked urgent out of the envelope. He read it and then read it again. He looked up at Harry. "It's from the old man. Allan Pinkerton says he never heard of a Mrs. Hannah Kinchman. She never worked for the Philadelphia office."

"Hannah Kinchman?" Clearly surprised, Harry stared back at Oliver. "How do you happen to know Johnny Lewis's sister?"

CHAPTER TWENTY-FIVE

Miss Battaile's boarding house was a brick fortress of respectability. A maid opened the door to Oliver.

"I'm sorry, sir. Mrs. Kinchman isn't at home."

"Can you tell me when you expect her back?"

"She's usually home for supper at seven-thirty, sir."

"Let me speak to your employer, please."

Whereas Kitty Putnam looked like a school marm and dressed the part, Miss Battaile, with her false golden ringlets and hugely bustled dress of purple and pink stripes, looked like an elderly harlot. Nevertheless, she gazed at Oliver sternly. "We do not give out information about our lady guests to strange gentlemen."

"Mrs. Kinchman happens to be employed by me."

"Then you can speak with her during business hours."

"She hasn't shown up for work in several days."

Mrs. Battaile pursed her rouged lips. "Mrs. Kinchman seems a respectable young lady. I know how it is when a man employs a pretty young woman with no protector. Perhaps you have given her good reason to avoid you."

Instead of replying in the manner that rose to his lips, Oliver left the house. Stalking past the hitching post he consulted his timepiece. It was now almost three-o'clock. If he returned to the boarding house by seven and kept watch, he might catch Hannah at supper. Then again, he might not. He pulled at his collar.

He wasn't surprised to learn that Hannah was more than she seemed and less than she'd claimed. According to Harry Barnett, she was the younger sister of the Lewis Brothers. Oliver remembered the trio of bankrobbers well--three doomed young men with blond moustaches, daredevil eyes and fast guns.

A posse of vigilantes had broken into the jail where Harry and Oliver had incarcerated the Lewises for the night. The ugly episode was one of many in his career as a Pinkerton that he would prefer to forget.

Hannah Kinchman would have been about ten when her brothers were lynched. Just what was she up to now? Nothing good where he was concerned. A cold fury rose up in him. There had been nothing that he or Harry could have done to save the Lewises from that enraged posse. If the woman thought by worming her way into his employ she could injure him or his, she was mistaken.

He had been striding down the brick walk so preoccupied by his thoughts. He was about to step off the curb when he was nearly toppled by a youngster racing around the corner on a Velocipede. As he dusted himself off he felt the back of his neck tingle.

Instead of crossing the street, he rounded the corner and stepped behind a tall hedge. A moment later a familiar looking young man in a box jacket and straw boater walked past. Oliver seized him by the throat and dragged him into a shadowy gap between two row houses.

"Why are you following me?"

"Arggg..." As the young man struggled, Oliver stared into his reddened face. He'd seen him before.

After giving his captive an extra shake, he loosened his grip. "You're the railroad attendant who served Nutwell, Rubman and Magruder dinner the night their car was sabotaged."

Cyrus Roe nodded in frantic agreement and sagged against the brick wall at his back. He coughed several times and then straightened his crumpled celluloid collar and string tie. "I wasn't really following you."

"You were. Doing a bad job of it, too."

"I merely wished to speak to you."

"You could have come to my house."

"I did, but you weren't home. When I saw you coming out of Miss Battaile's, I hurried to catch you up."

Oliver didn't like the way Roe's puppy dog eyes never gave you a straight look. On the other hand, maybe he was taking his fury at Hannah Kinchman out on an innocent young man. "What did you want to speak to me about?"

"I saw the fellow I described to you, the tall one with the diamond who made remarks about Magruder."

"Did you?"

"I even found out his name. It's Jaggard. I've seen him driving around town in a fancy carriage with that actress, Sarah Bernhardt. She's in town for a play."

"Did you learn more of Jaggard than you've told me?"

Roe's prideful expression dimmed. "No, but I could. If you'll give me leave, I'll follow him in my spare time."

"If the way you dogged me is a sample of your skill at following people, you'd be better off in church." Oliver picked up the straw boater he'd knocked from Roe's head and handed it over. "Look, I'm sorry I roughed you up."

"It doesn't matter," Roe said, though clearly from his resentful tone, it did. "I'd do a good job for you. Jaggard would never suspect me tailing him. I'm not asking for money. I just want to show you what I can do."

"You want to play at being a detective?"

"I won't be playing. It's to my advantage to find out who wrecked that private car. Until it's known, everybody who worked that night is under suspicion. Let me find out what I can about Jaggard. You won't be sorry, I swear it!"

Why not, Oliver asked himself. After sending Roe on his way, he headed home. When he arrived, Chloe and Mrs. Milawney were leaving. Laura had kindly arranged for them to see a late afternoon performance of "The Two Orphans" with Kate Claxton.

For half an hour he paced about the first floor of the town-house asking himself how he should handle Hannah Kinchman. Was it possible that she was behind these attacks on him? He took out the newspaper interview with his cousin that she'd left for him and read it through. He read the last paragraph twice. In it Griff named Ben Magruder as the officer responsible for the deaths of thirty Confederate prisoners.

The doorbell clanged. Oliver looked through the window, then hurried into the hall and flung open the door.

"Laura, is that you?"

She lifted the veil from her face. "Are you going to let me in? Or are you going to keep me standing out here on the stoop so your neighbors can gossip?"

He followed her into the parlor. The neighbors could have no idea of her identity. Laura's wide-brimmed hat and heavy veil covered her face completely.

Dropping the hat onto a chair, she smoothed back a strand of golden hair and smiled at him. "Alone at last!"

CHAPTER TWENTY-SIX

"**L**aura, why have you come? Is Griff all right?"

"Griff is as fine as he's been since the damned war."

"Good. It's lucky you should visit at this moment. I have a question for you. Did a man named Magruder visit Griff in the recent past?"

"Magruder, Magruder." She tapped her pretty, pointed chin. "Oh yes, of course. That awful man came to the house a couple of months ago. Griff had him thrown out."

"What did they argue about?"

"Heaven's, I've no idea. I didn't come here to talk about your Mr. Magruder." Laura ran her hand along the settee's polished mahogany head-rail. "You old sentimentalist. You haven't replaced any of your aunt's furniture. I remember in the old days how I used to sit right here with you and Griff, drinking tea and eating cookies and just flirting something outrageous."

"I remember that, too." All too easily, he called up an image of Laura as she'd been then--an angel of light in her blue gown and dainty slippers. "You were the prettiest girl in the world."

"And now?" she said quickly. "What am I now?"

"Why, you've hardly changed."

"Oh haven't I?" Her tone was suddenly caustic. "Oh Ollie, when we were young, I was a different person. I looked at your cousin and saw a young Apollo."

"So did I."

"There's nothing godlike about him now. The war destroyed

everything for us, didn't it?" Laura faced him. "I'm here because I think its time we were honest with each other. For the past seventeen years I've been married to a man who is little better than a vegetable. Oh, a handsome vegetable, to be sure, one who speaks and talks. But not a man, Oliver. Griff hasn't been a man since he came back from Point Lookout. I'm married to a eunuch."

She flew at him, her hands outstretched, her eyes moist and pleading. "All I ever wanted was children. That's only what every normal woman wants. I'm the same age as you. I haven't much time left. Oliver, when I knew you all those years ago, I loved you in my way. But you never put yourself forward. You never tried to take me away from Griff. Perhaps if you had, things would have been different. Perhaps I might even have married you."

He shook his head. He'd had nothing to offer Laura, and Griff had seemed to have everything. Even now, Griff could provide her with a far more comfortable life.

Tears sparkled in her eyes. "Life is so filled with cruel ironies. You're the man I had hoped Griff would be."

"You're not seeing me as I am."

"Yes!" She gave a breathless little laugh that was half sob. "You've stood up to life. You're not weak, above all, you're not weak. I know you cared for me. Is there anything left of those feelings?"

She put her hands on either side of his face and drew his head down so that her breath feathered his lips. Through her corset, he felt the warmth of her body. Her breasts, behind the thin silk of her bodice, brushed his shirtfront. As a boy he'd dreamt of touching her intimately. "Laura, why have you come here?"

"Haven't you guessed by now? We have the rest of the afternoon together here alone. Give me my heart's desire, Oliver. Give me a child."

"Laura!"

"You've had a mistress and she's given you an illegitimate child. Oh yes, I know who Chloe's mother was. You can't keep that sort of thing a secret in a town like Baltimore. The life you've led--you've probably made love to dozens of women."

"That has nothing to do with you."

"Oh, you men! You think there are good women and bad women. But all women want love. You've given your mistress a child, why can't you do the same for me? If you'll only think about it, you'll see it makes perfect sense. Since you came back to town, I've thought of nothing but this. You're the ideal father for the child I want to have."

Oliver groaned.

"I know what you're thinking. You always were too noble for your own good. But Griff won't be hurt. You're his nearest male relative. If I had a child with you, it would be almost as if I'd had one with him. Nothing could make more sense."

"Griff knows you're here? He sent you?"

"Griff won't object once its a fait accompli. His family name means more to him than anything. Oliver, we're adults. Believe me, what we do will hurt no one." Her hands tightened. She fastened her lips to his. Her kiss was warm, urgent, desperate.

Oliver felt his body tighten. Involuntarily, his hands clenched Laura's shoulders. He turned his head.

Laura wouldn't let him go. Laying her cheek on his chest, she whispered, "Take me upstairs. Show me your room. Show me your bed. I'll do anything you want. I'll be a better woman for you than Chloe's mother ever was."

"Laura, I can't. Griff and I are cousins. We shared too much as boys for me to share his wife now."

"Oh!" She pushed him away and crossed her arms tight over her breasts. "There wouldn't be any sharing involved. Griff doesn't want me, hasn't wanted me in ages."

"You marriage is unconsummated?"

"It's been consummated, I suppose, if you really want to call it that. Foolishly, I agreed to marry him just after he escaped that prison camp and before he recovered his health. Then, when he felt better, he fumbled at me a few times. It was never. . ." She hesitated. "I was relieved when he stopped, and I didn't encourage him to try again. Oh, I was young and stupid. Then, as the years passed, I realized I was never going to have children." She snatched up her hat. Clutching it between her hands, she faced him tearfully. "All I wanted was a child. That's the only reason I came here, the only reason I humbled and humiliated myself like this." Laura ran from the room.

Stunned, Oliver followed her, but he was too late. He listened to the echo of the slammed door. I'm a fool, he thought, a complete fool. Dazedly, he walked back into the parlor. It seemed to echo with Laura's entreaties. Choking frustration rose up in him.

The clock on the mantel struck six. He remembered that he had planned to set up a watch outside Miss Battaile's to try and catch Hannah Kinchman. All that seemed to belong to another life.

After pouring himself a large whiskey, he went out into the garden. It was that time of the early evening when the worst of the day's heat had abated and long shadows traced patterns on the gravel path.

As he sipped his whiskey, his mind traveled back in time. Behind the tree where he leaned he seemed to hear the sound of Laura's laughter mixed with his own and Griff's. My God, had this encounter with Laura shaken him so badly that he was hallucinating? His eyes narrowed. That wasn't ghostly laughter, but the very real rustle of someone moving furtively over the grass.

After setting his glass down, he moved stealthily around the tree in time to seize a slender neck and pinion the body it belonged to against his. "What the hell?"

"Please!"

His hand raked down the length of a cotton-covered arm and felt the shape of a derringer concealed beneath the material. He pried it away, half ripping the sleeve off Hannah Kinchman's dress.

CHAPTER TWENTY-SEVEN

He shoved her against the tree trunk. While she struggled for breath, he checked her derringer. It was an old fashioned single shot model, impossible to unload easily.

"That's mine. You have no right!"

Burying his fingers deep in her coiled hair so that she let out a little yip, he dragged her face close to his. "Don't talk to me about rights. I know who you are. Your real name is Lewis."

He felt her body stiffen. "Why did you come to Baltimore? Why did you lie your way into my employ? What did you plan by sneaking into my garden with this?" He threw her gun over his shoulder and heard it land somewhere in the bushes.

"Nothing. I always carry that derringer. I'm a woman alone. I need some protection."

"Liar! You came here tonight planning to shoot me."

"No, no, I came to report..."

"You have a Navy Colt at home, don't you? Maybe one you inherited from your thieving brothers? If you grew up a Lewis, you know how to ride a horse, and I've learned your talent for disguise. It was you who took a pot shot at me on the road between here and the Rubman house."

"I...I..."

"You dressed up like a man, hid behind some trees and took a pop at me!" He shook her.

Instead of admitting the truth, she struck out at him and tried to wriggle free. She was surprisingly strong, but he used his body to pin her hard against the tree.

"Be quiet!"

"Let me go! You've no right!"

When she continued struggling and fussing, rage swirled through him. He took her lips with his and ground her mouth against her teeth. There was nothing friendly in the kiss. It was an attack.

She went limp against him.

He drew back. Though the darkness hid his face, he knew it was red with mortification. He hadn't meant to kiss her like that. The last thing he wanted with this damnable woman was sex. The kiss had come, at least in part, from his frustration about Laura.

"Just like a man," Hannah hissed. "What did you think you'd gain by forcing yourself on me? Did you think I'd throw my arms around you? Did you think I'd been longing to kiss the man responsible for killing my brothers?"

"At least it got the truth out of you? You came here to assassinate me, didn't you?"

"If I'd really wanted you dead, you'd have been in your coffin days ago."

"Are you still denying that you took a shot at me?"

Her gaze dropped. "After you turned me away so rudely that afternoon, I was determined to convince you to hire me. I followed you to Felicia Rubman's house. I hid and shot at you. My plan was to come to you later with the gun and discarded clothing, claiming I'd tracked them down as a favor to you. I hoped you'd be so impressed by my detecting skills that you'd hire me."

"Hogwash! You wanted to put a bullet into me."

"Have it your own way, but the moment I pulled the trigger I realized it was a mistake. I'm not a killer. That's why I turned tail and ran instead of finishing you off the way you deserved."

"It was you who shot at me in the park, too."

"No, no, I swear! That wasn't me!"

"You don't know what truth is! You forged that damned

letter from Allan Pinkerton and came here to Baltimore for the express purpose of harming me. Or maybe, once you snooped out my situation, you decided to get at me through my family. Did you sneak into the garden tonight in hopes of finding Chloe?"

She looked shocked. "You can't believe I'd ever want to hurt a child! My God, after what I've been through? After what my life has been? I was hardly older than your daughter when my brothers were murdered. It killed my mother. I had to raise myself and my little brother alone. Do you have any idea what it's like to be an orphaned child, utterly alone and destitute? Thank God my dead brother's ladyfriend took me under her wing. She was an actress. That's how I learned to earn my bread."

"You blame me for that?"

"Shouldn't I?" She glared at him. "It was you and your partner who put my brothers in that cracker box of a jail. It was you and your partner who were responsible for their safety."

"Your brothers had stirred up such a hornet's nest in that town, there was nothing we could do to protect them. We were miles away when they were dragged out of their cells and hanged."

"You shouldn't have been miles away! You should have been there protecting them. They were just boys!"

Oliver was silent. He had been a boy then, too--just nineteen. The little Missouri town where he and Harry had jailed the Lewises had seemed peaceable. It had been a bad miscalculation.

"As if that wasn't enough," she went on bitterly, "you put Johnny in jail and threw the key away."

"Johnny? You mean your bloodthirsty little brother?

"He's hardly more than a child. All right, he boasted in a bar that he was going to hunt you down. It was just talk. But the Pinkertons have the Philadelphia police in their pockets. The morning after Johnny behaved like a fool they burst into our rooms and dragged him off to jail on some trumped-up charge. They aren't going to let him out until the Pinkerton's give their say-so."

"Lying to me, taking shots at me from behind a bush, is that how you plan to get your brother out of the clink?"

"I was just desperate. I apologize for what I did. It was stupid and wrong."

"Why did you want to work for me?"

"I thought I might be able to find a way to persuade you to help me with Johnny."

"What you really mean is that you wanted to get close to me so you could blackmail me."

All this time Hannah had been meeting his angry gaze unflinchingly. "Laura Singleton. I saw her leave the house just now. I've seen the two of you together before. There's an atmosphere between the two of you."

"So you've been following me, watching my house?" Oliver was outraged.

"I haven't cheated you. I've been working on the Rubman investigation."

"You're far more interested in investigating me. Do you accuse me of having an affair with my cousin's wife?"

"No."

"Of course you do. You want to blackmail me."

"No, I've changed my mind about that."

"Then what do you want?"

"To help you solve this case. I had thought to make myself so useful to you that you'd gladly help me get justice for my brother." Ignoring his disbelieving snort, she hurried on. "I've been doing a good job for you so far, haven't I?"

"Obviously, from that little scene in the park the other day, you've succeeded in worming your way into Penrose's confidence. I'll give you that."

"It was I who found out about the affair between Penrose's wife and Enoch Rubman. Now I know more. I know the reason why she killed herself. She had syphilis."

"Syphilis!"

"I also know there's something very odd about the relationship she had with her husband."

"There's something odd about the relationship you're de-veloping with Penrose. I saw you posing for him. Have you be-come his artist's model?"

"Yes."

"Are you posing naked for him?"

Her mouth opened slightly. She looked surprised by the question. "I am."

"That was never part of your job description, Mrs. Kinch-man. Our professional association is ended."

"Why? Because you're responsible for my brothers getting hanged or because I took my clothes off in front of a man I'm not married to?"

"You can run naked through the Market Exchange at high noon, for all I care."

"Has anyone ever told you that you are a narrow-minded prude?"

"I've been called many things."

"None of them would surprise me." She straightened her spine, her angry eyes drilling into his. "All right, I'll leave and you won't see my face again. But I want my property back. Please return my gun."

Oliver snorted. "That'll be a cold day in hell."

She darted toward the row of bushes where he'd thrown it, but he stopped her and marched her to the gate.

"You'll regret this!" she threatened after he'd locked her out of his garden.

CHAPTER TWENTY-EIGHT

"I'm surprised to see you here, Cousin Ollie." Laura, gowned in a lavender dress with a high neck, locked her hands primly at her waist.

"I'm sorry to disturb you this morning, but I must speak with Griff."

"About what?" Horror crossed her face.

He realized she feared he meant to tell Griff about her failed attempt at seduction. "No! It has to do with my investigation. I need to ask him a few questions."

"Griff is in the garden, as usual."

Oliver tried to think of something to say. But there was nothing to say. He found his cousin seated in the same grape arbor where he'd discovered him on his earlier visit.

"This is an unlooked for pleasure, cousin. What brings you to my humble sanctuary at this early hour? Not that it matters, the earliness I mean. I'm always awake at first light. I'm very sensitive to light and its many qualities. Impaired vision, like every other compromising condition, bestows certain benefits. Over the years I've become a connoisseur of shadows."

Oliver sat down on the stone bench opposite. "I met your friends, Primm and Wiseby the other day."

Griff's mask of calm broke into a slight smile. "So I heard. The war keeps tapping us on the shoulder with skeleton fingers, doesn't it?"

"How did you hear? Did Primm or Wiseby come see you again?"

"Marshal Rackley told me he rescued you from an choleric mob at Kernan's."

"Rackley?"

"I hear the surprise in your voice, Ollie. Don't you know how consequential the Singleton family is in these parts? When Grandfather ruled the roost here at Zephyrus, the Commissioner of Police came around every month to pay homage. Rackley knows his appointment depends on the good will of families like the Singletons. He's just carrying on the tradition."

"Are you telling me he takes orders from you?"

Griff laughed. "Those palmy days of privilege are forever finished. I haven't been a worthy custodian of the family riches, I fear. Rackley still pays his respects, but it's a mere formality. Money is power, Oliver, as I'm sure you've observed."

"What are you saying, Griff? I thought Grandfather left you a large fortune."

"So he did, but treasure has a way of dwindling when you've made unlucky investments. I don't know why I'm boring you with this nonsense. Why did you come?"

"Two months ago you gave an interview to the Sun. In it you mentioned Magruder's name. Later, he came to see you."

"How did you know that? Who told you?" Griff's expression turned accusatory. "You wormed it out of Laura, didn't you?"

"I don't think she realized you'd prefer me not to know."

"There is nothing to know. Apparently, the brute was in Baltimore on business and saw the article. He came to the house and I refused to see him, that's all."

Laura had said that they'd argued. "And you never met him again?"

"Never."

"Yet, at one time you had a close relationship with him. According to Primm and Wiseby, he dragged you up to the guard house often for private tete-a-tetes."

"To torture and abuse me. I'd hardly call that a close relationship."

According to Primm and Wiseby, you are the only one who

escaped from Point Lookout with a whole skin that night. They think somebody told Magruder about the planned escape. He posted extra guards who shot all the other men in your break-out party."

"I've never been certain what happened to the others. There was so much confusion. We became separated almost immediately. It was sheer luck that I survived."

"Amazing, isn't it?"

Griff glared. "Did Primm and Wiseby dare suggest that I betrayed our escape plans that dreadful night?"

"Not at all. They talked about how much they hated Magruder. Could they have been behind his death?"

Griff sniffed. "Those fools would blow his brains out on the street. They wouldn't have the forethought to arrange an accidental train wreck."

That was Oliver's opinion as well. "Can you think of anyone else from your Point Lookout days who might have wanted Magruder dead?"

"Dozens. But most of them are six feet under."

"If you did know the assassin, you wouldn't tell me, would you?"

"I'm glad Magruder is dead. I'm only sorry his death throes weren't longer and more excruciating. I regret he didn't have to spend years feeling his vitality drain away while his inheritance dwindled and his wife looked at him with disenchanted eyes. Now, that's truly a cruel fate."

Oliver felt his gut twist. "Griff, for God's sake man, it's not as bad as that, is it?"

"No, of course it isn't." Griff laughed lightly. "I'm dramatizing. I've always dramatized myself. It's the mark of the righteously self-centered. Forgive me, Ollie." He lifted a pale hand. "Say nothing about bad investments to Laura. I've magnified that, as well." He made another airy gesture. "I've lost a few of Grandfather's dollars on the market, it's true, but there's plenty to see us through. I wouldn't want her to think otherwise. It would kill me to lose her, you know. She's all I've got."

Oliver said goodbye and walked toward the maze of yew hedges bordering Griff's extensive gardens. Laura intercepted him. "Sneaking off?"

"I didn't want to disturb you."

"You always were terribly considerate, weren't you? Even when you were a boy you were so considerate you never even tried to steal me away from Griff. If you had, I might never have married him."

"Believe me, Griff has made you a far better husband than I would have done."

"How can that be true when Griff is no husband at all? Do you say it because of what Quantrill did to your family? That was terrible, but if I'd been at your side, I could have helped you heal. You might never have become a lawman and lived this terrible, wandering, violent life."

"Laura," he said gently, "when I was a boy I craved adventure. The truth is that I don't regret the life I've led--even despite the bad dreams it sometimes gives me. It would never have worked between us. I couldn't have given you what you needed. I'm not the man you imagine. In my way I'm just as selfish and weak as all the other men who've disappointed you."

Her mouth turned down. "That's just a mealy-mouthed way of saying I couldn't have given you what you needed, isn't it? Did Chloe's mother give you what you needed?"

"Marietta has nothing to do with us."

Laura seized his hand. "What if Chloe isn't yours? She mightn't be, you know. With a woman like her mother, you can't be sure. If you were to give me a child, you could be sure it was really yours."

Oliver pulled free. "Of course Chloe is my child. Excuse me, Laura, I must go." He stepped around her and walked quickly out to the gravel drive. All the way he was aware of her bitter green eyes boring into his back.

Once again, Hannah knocked on Aurelia Burnside Davies'

front door. The thud of her knuckles rang hollow, and there was no answer. Flora Penrose's crusty older sister was not at home. Hannah looked to her left. Outside the shade of a few spindly trees the sun beat down on the brick sidewalks fiercely. A faint odor of horse urine rose from the Belgian block paving the street.

The other houses were shuttered, their curtains drawn tight against the heat. Perspiration pooled between Hannah's breasts and under her stays. She supposed she should give up on this fool's errand. Indeed, perhaps she should leave Baltimore altogether. Certainly, she'd received no encouragement from Oliver Redcastle to stay on.

But a hard nut of determination wouldn't let her leave this unfinished business. She wanted to show Oliver Redcastle that he was wrong. She wanted to rub his haughty nose in his wrongness.

After unlatching a tall wooden gate, she entered the back garden. It contained only a few neglected rosebushes and scraggly hollyhocks. A cracked reflecting globe stood on a pedestal in a patch of gravel. A rickety grape arbor sheltered a rusty chair.

Hannah tapped on the back door. It was in poor repair, the wood partially rotted around the rusty, old fashioned lock. She gave it a little push and it creaked open. Her pulse raced. She stuck her head through the opening and called out, "Mrs. Davies?" No answer. The house was definitely empty, and empty house's couldn't tell tales. Or could they?

Ten minutes later she had made a fruitless circuit of the kitchen, dining room and small parlor. Save the intriguing portrait of Flora Penrose, she had found nothing of interest. With Flora's eyes seeming to watch her reproachfully, she mounted the steps to the second floor.

It was easy enough to pick out Aurelia's bedroom as the other rooms were either layered with dust or being used as storerooms. As Hannah inspected the other woman's closets and looked under her bed, she asked herself what she would do if Aurelia Burnside Davies came home and caught her trespassing.

With no satisfactory answer, she opened all the drawers on a tall oak bureau. Beneath a pile of frayed under things, she found a journal bound in cracked leather. When she opened it, she discovered a packet of letters tied in lavender ribbon. They were from Flora Penrose.

CHAPTER TWENTY-NINE

A day later Hannah mailed Flora Penrose's letters back to her sister. More than likely Aurelia had already discovered them missing. Hannah hoped she wouldn't guess the thief.

When the package was safely on its way, she proceeded to Beacher Penrose's studio. It was to be her last appointment with the artist and one of the reasons why she hadn't left Baltimore yet.

As she mounted the steps to the studio, she felt a warm glow suffuse her limbs. It wasn't just the climb. When she posed for Beacher she felt as if she had opened a door and crossed into a different dimension. Once her clothes were shed, she was a new made creature, a butterfly emancipated from its dull cocoon.

The very thought of his appreciative gaze stirred tender erotic currents within her. They were all the more delicious because she did not expect that she and Beacher would ever make love. Indeed, now that she had read his wife's letters to Aurelia, she knew they would not.

Many would scorn her because she had posed naked for a man who was not her husband. Yet, as she crouched on the floor before Beacher, she had never felt more detached from her physical self. She seemed to see her body through the prism of the artist's vision. It was a view purely esthetic, free of all that was gross.

He greeted her with a smile that lit his beautiful eyes. She felt his pleasure reflected back to him in her own gaze. He said,

"I've been pacing up and down waiting for you this last half hour."

"Aren't you working on other projects?"

"Several, but lately I've been able to concentrate on nothing but Hespere. That's what I've named our statue, yours and mine, Hespere, the goddess of evening who guarded the golden apples beyond the western ocean. An appropriate goddess for an American sculptor, don't you think? She's nearly finished." He pointed to a sheet-covered shape.

"May I see her?"

"Not yet. Not until you've posed for me today."

Quickly, Hannah undressed and assumed the correct folded posture. Yet, she didn't go into her usual trancelike state. There were too many things to consider. Uppermost in her mind were the revelations of the letters.

According to Flora's letters to her sister, Beacher had never consummated their marriage. They had slept in separate bedrooms and lived more like brother and sister than husband and wife. At first, naive child that she'd been at the time of her marriage, Flora had accepted this arrangement. Then she'd been seduced by Enoch Rubman.

"Oh sister," she'd written. "It's as if blinders have fallen from my eyes. I'm so ashamed! And yet. . ."

Hannah was not an innocent. In her career on the stage she had known several handsome male actors who preferred lovers of their own sex. But Beacher she suspected of being something else, something rare, a man who had entirely sublimated his sexuality in an esthetic sensibility so heightened that it made the ordinary commerce of the flesh impossible for him. Poor Flora.

Beacher sighed. "It's finished," he said. "You may look if you wish."

She struggled out of her crouch and reached for her robe. Sharp pains stabbed at her legs and back. But as her gaze fell on Beacher's work, she forgot her pain. "It's beautiful!"

"It's not finished yet. I still need to mix pumice with water for its final buffing."

"It's already so beautiful that it takes my breath." And it did. It was as if his hand had melted away a shell of stone and freed a creature of such grace that the sight of it left Hannah blinking in astonishment. Hespere knelt on a bed of leaves and flowers in an attitude of supplication. From her outstretched hands tumbled a half dozen apples, each exquisitely carved.

"She looks incredibly alive. I almost expect to see her breathe." Hannah felt as if Beacher had captured her essence, her hidden self and immortalized it. "Is that really me?"

"No," he replied sharply. His eyes remained fixed on his work. "It's the ideal of beauty that you inspired in my hands. Beauty is like a sunset cloud floating above a mud puddle. It may take its matter from that dirty water, but its essential nature is something entirely apart."

Hannah pretended to pout. "It's unkind to compare me to a mud puddle. Surely the rose you paint is even more beautiful than your representation because, after all, the rose is real. It scents the air, which is something a painting can't do."

Beacher shook his head. "The rose is corruptible. It's loveliness fades and grows ugly. My painting catches the ideal of its essence. Beauty is merely an idea. It's the artist's task to capture that idea and preserve it in time, at least so far as he is able. Something of you, perhaps the best part of you, lives in Hespere. Like a god, I have breathed eternal life into that something."

She felt that what he said was true. Still, his smug self-satisfaction stung her. "But we are not ideas. We are human beings. Our flesh may be corruptible, but it's through our flesh that we express the noblest as well as the worst of our impulses. Love is expressed through the flesh. You must know that, since you've been married." She touched his shoulder and felt the hard bone and sinew beneath his cotton smock. A shock of memory and longing stirred her. Gilbert's shoulder had felt like this, and she'd loved her runaway husband to distraction.

Beacher pulled away from her and turned his back. "Your robe is hanging open. You should dress."

"Why should that matter? You've seen me naked."

"It's different when I'm painting or sculpting. There's no embarrassment, no ugly carnal thoughts. I see only the purity of the shapes, the light and the shadow."

"Are you having carnal thoughts about me now?" Hannah asked curiously. She acknowledged to herself that she had half fallen in love with this peculiar man. Despite everything, if Beacher were to take her into his arms now, she would submit-- gladly.

"Cover your breasts."

"Why?" Defiantly, she pulled the robe apart and let it puddle on the floor at her feet. "Is there something about them that offends you?"

"Yes! They're ugly! I can't stand the sight of them. Cover yourself at once and leave!"

After reading Flora's letters, Hannah knew she shouldn't be surprised or offended. Still, she was appalled by the snarl twisting his handsome features. The hurt woman in her reacted.

"You've just spent hours sculpting my naked body. How can it suddenly offend you?"

He pointed at the statue. "Hespere's breasts are hidden, her limbs are smooth and perfect. She's not like a real woman, only like what a woman should be and never is."

Hannah put on the robe. As her fingers fumbled to tie the garment closed, he exclaimed, "You gawk at me as if I were a freak. But it's you who are the freak. Women with there pretty faces lure men into believing that what's hidden beneath their garments is equally lovely. But it isn't, it isn't! It's horrible!"

Hannah lost her temper. "Women are made of flesh not marble. Their bodies are not meant to be like the bodies of young boys. You painted your wife to look like a naked boy, but I know that she wasn't boyish. I've seen another painting of her in her sister's house, one that resembled the real woman. Flora was built like a normal woman, with breasts and hips and thighs--all the bodily things a woman must have to bear the children given to them by husbands who are real men."

"Leave!"

"Is that why your wife had an affair with another man, contracted syphilis from him and hung herself? Did you turn away from her in disgust as you are turning away from me? Did you kill her with your neglect?"

Beacher's face flamed red. As he stood clenching his fists and grinding his teeth, Hannah felt sure that he was going to strike her down. Instead, his burning eyes filled with tears. He crumpled onto a chair and covered his face with his hands. "Oh God," he cried, "Oh God, I am cursed! I drove my wife to infidelity and then to suicide. Now, you have found me out. You are the angel of retribution come to accuse me! It is I who am the monster!"

Shocked to her core, Hannah moved forward and clasped Beacher's shaking shoulders. "I'm so sorry," she whispered. "So sorry. Forgive me. I should never have said that. Forgive me, please."

He only shuddered more deeply and drew away from her as if her touch scalded him. "Get out!"

CHAPTER THIRTY

Mrs. Milawney poked her head into the dining room. "There's that young man, Mr. Roe, to see you."

Oliver folded his napkin. "He's paying his visits bright and early."

Chloe swallowed the last of her poached egg and smiled shyly. He smiled back, pleased that her cheeks were not so pale this morning. Now that the summer was more advanced, she was sleeping through the night and able to spend more time out of doors. Yesterday she'd taken her dolls for a buggy ride in the park. Mrs. Pringle hadn't been among them, and Oliver hadn't been able to keep himself from asking, "Is Mrs. Pringle still sick?"

Chloe had nodded solemnly. What had happened to the doll, he wondered. Was he ever to see Chloe play with his gift? If he had any sense, he'd stop thinking about it.

"This Mr. Roe values his time more than yours," Mrs. Milawney huffed. "Shall I tell him to come back at a decent hour?"

"I'll see him in my study."

A few minutes later Cyrus Roe stepped into the room clutching his straw boater. "I wanted to speak to you before I report for work, sir. I hope I'm not interrupting your breakfast."

Roe launched into an enthusiastic account of his activities the night before. "I tracked Jake Jaggard down at his hotel and followed him between the hours of six and eleven p.m."

"Did he see you?"

"No, no!" Roe pushed back a lock of brown hair. "I stayed in the shadows and mixed with the crowd, just the way you advised. He never saw me! I swear it."

"Where did Jaggard go?"

Roe consulted a notebook. "He spent a little over an hour dining at Kelly's Raw Oyster Bar and Saloon on Eutaw Street. From there he went to a wine shop on Monument. He stayed a long time in the wine shop, a little over an hour. After that he met friends and went with them to The French Froliques near North Avenue and then The White Elephant."

The Elephant was an East Baltimore hot spot and The Froliques a low class theater. Oliver thought Jaggard's patrician tastes must be slipping.

Roe continued his report. "When they left The White Elephant they went to Barnums where they repaired to a private room. I waited around until eleven. One of the waiters told me that if they stayed true to form they might play cards until three in the morning and finish off a dozen bottles of their most expensive spirits."

"Jaggard fancies himself a connoisseur of fine vintages, so I'm not..." Instead of finishing his sentence, Oliver frowned and leaned forward. "Is this wine shop you mentioned next to the Monument National bank?"

"Yes, sir. Right next door."

"Did you see anybody else go in while Jaggard was there?"

Roe frowned down at his notes. "One fellow. He went in shortly after Jaggard and came out just before." Roe described him and Oliver listened intently.

"Good work. I appreciate your efforts."

Roe flushed with pleasure. "Is there any importance to what I saw. Has it helped you?"

"I can't be sure yet, but quite possibly it has."

"Does that mean you'll take me on as an apprentice detective? I can't tell you what it would mean to me!"

"I'll definitely give it some thought."

Two hours later, Oliver rapped on Gentleman Jake Jaggard's hotel door. There was no reply. After glancing in both directions down the blessedly empty corridor, he let himself in with a skeleton key. He found Jaggard snoring next to a pretty strawberry blond.

Oliver emptied the full pitcher on the washstand over the two of them. Jaggard bolted into a sitting position. As if by magic, the derringer he apparently kept under his pillow, leapt into his hand. Clutching the sheet to her breasts, the girl let out an operatic arpeggio of shrieks.

Ignoring the prostitute, Oliver said, "Put the gun away, Jake, and tell your lady friend to get dressed and leave. We've some talking to do."

Despite his nakedness, Jake assumed an imperious expression. "This is outrageous, Redcastle! How dare you insult this lovely lady who just happened to fall asleep at my side! Isn't an honest man safe in his own bed in this hick town? I shall have to report you to the authorities."

"Cut the apple butter. I know the group who's leasing Wiley's Fine Import Wines & Spirits. I've got a good hunch why they're in business. Is that a hunch you'd like me to report to the authorities?"

Jaggard lowered his derringer and turned to his shivering bedmate. "Maggie, my dear, it's been delightful, but the time has come for us to part. That's a good girl."

Fifteen minutes later, Maggie had dressed, accepted the folded bills Jake pressed into her hand and sidled out the door. Jake himself had slipped into a handsome silk dressing gown and ordered a "razzle-dazzle" from room service, a drink consisting of equal parts brandy, absinthe and ginger ale.

He sipped it in the sitting room and glowered at Oliver. "What the devil do you mean crashing about in my room?"

Oliver smiled sweetly and sank into a silk-covered armchair. While admiring Jake's lordly show of outrage, he felt sure he held the cards. "A few nights back, Danny Coy tried to knock my block off in an alley."

"You don't say so." Jake flicked a bit of lint from one of the lapels on his robe. "Did he succeed?"

"He did not. But even after I showed him his error in judgment, Coy stuck to me like a burr, even trailing me on a little job I needed to do."

"Fascinating. What has this to do with me, pray tell?"

"I haven't been able to figure out why Coy took such a close interest in me and my activities. He claimed that he made himself my shadow because he was paid to keep a watch on the bank. Somehow that didn't seem right. Now I've got a new idea. He's not only collecting a paycheck for guarding the bank. He's working for you, too, isn't he?"

"Dear boy, I don't know what you're talking about."

"Jake, you should be on the stage with Bernhardt. According to city records, Wiley's Wines opened six months ago. The proprietor is one Fenton Gambrill. That's one of Aldo Wheeler's aliases. You and Aldo have worked together on a half dozen bank and jewelry store jobs. It was you and Wheeler who blasted into Boston Union Bank and Trust. Three months earlier the two of you opened a French restaurant which just happened to have a common wall with the bank."

"You have an overactive imagination and no proof that either Aldo or I was involved in any illegal activity. Neither of our names was on the lease of that restaurant."

"Very clever. Harry and I were never able to recover the money or close the case, but we knew it was you who masterminded that robbery. It had your signature."

"Sour grapes, Oliver. I thought you were above that sort of pettiness."

"Jake, you're as slick as axle grease, but this time I've caught you. You're in cahoots with Aldo Wheeler again, aren't you?"

Jake studied his fingernails. "Actually, that shop is being run by a nephew of Aldo's. The poor young lad is trying to become a legitimate businessman. Out of concern for an old friend, I've taken a small interest. It's a good fit. As you know, I've always enjoyed the grape."

"The set of you are scheming to get into that bank."

"Nonsense. You've spent too many formative years with the

Pinkertons. It's turned you into a cynic. There's no common wall between our shop and the bank. They're two independent structures. It's sheer coincidence that the shop is close to a financial institution."

"The only thing worse than lying is getting caught at it, Jaggard. Coy is working for you, isn't he?"

"What if he is? Since he's already guarding the bank, it's convenient for Aldo to employ him as a night watchman. A prosperous wine shop is an obvious target for thieves."

"He's a night watchman who takes his job very seriously. He was all over me just because I happened to spend some time looking into the window of that shop."

"What's it to you how seriously a street tough like Coy takes his job? You're not working for the Pinkertons anymore. Or are you?" Jaggard's eyes narrowed.

"I am a citizen of Baltimore. As such, I should report my suspicions to Marshal Rackley."

"Go ahead. Rackley will laugh at you."

That was probably true, Oliver thought, Rackley being a corrupt and thickheaded buffoon deeply enmeshed in his own nefarious schemes. It was even possible that Rackley was in Jaggard's pay.

Jake added, "If you were really foolish enough to tell Rackley a cock and bull story about a respectable man such as myself planning a bank robbery, it would have happened by now. What's your real reason for being here?"

"I need to make use of your skills, Jake. I want you to steal something for me."

Two hours past midnight the two men slipped into the alley behind the Eutaw hotel. Both were clothed head to foot in black. As Oliver glanced back at Jake, he had to admire the figure he cut. In his daytime dress he looked like an effete fop. In his working clothes his true personality emerged, and he looked like the internationally feared burglar he really was.

They melted into the shadows and stood gazing up at the window of the office that was their target. "Do you think you can climb that?"

"Easily. The tricky part will be getting through the window without alarming the guard they've posted."

"If your reputation means anything, you'll do that. If I'm lucky, the file folder will still be where I hid it," Oliver whispered.

"And if it's not?"

"Then I'll have to come up by the stairs, knock the guard over the head and tear the place apart."

"That's not my style, Ollie. If this folder you're after is still in that room, I'll find it for you and no one will guess the place has been touched."

"But..."

"I have my reputation to consider. Jake Jaggard never makes a bloody mess and never leaves a trail. Keep a lookout. If you smell trouble, whistle."

Like a dancer preparing for a performance, Jake flexed his shoulders and shifted his weight on the balls of his feet. Tools of his trade hung from a slotted leather belt on his waist. In one gloved hand he carried a length of rope attached to a three-pronged grappling hook. "Useful for quick exits," he had explained to Oliver.

"I'm grateful for this, Jaggard."

"Instead of ruining my morning with that damned freezing pitcher of water, you should simply have told me what you wanted. I'm always delighted to help out an old friend."

"I didn't realize we were old friends."

"We will be after tonight. After tonight, Ollie, we'll be partners in crime--my most prized relationship. Now, I'm off. Wish me luck."

Jaggard crossed the alley and began to scale the building. Oliver watched in awe as he found hand and footholds. The man's a damned bat, he thought.

Silently, Jake cut a hole in the windowpane large enough so

that he could unlock the window. The heavy wooden sash rattled faintly as he lifted it, but no alarm was raised. Jake slipped noiselessly inside.

Ten long minutes later he reappeared with a fat sheaf of papers tucked inside his belt.

CHAPTER THIRTY-ONE

Reluctant to awaken Chloe and Mrs. Milawney by coming in the front door of his house at this early hour, Oliver went around the side and quietly opened the garden gate. The sky had turned fuzzy gray. A light breeze fanned the leaves on the trees, which had the appearance of inky blurs in the uncertain light. The files he'd acquired from Jake rattled faintly inside his jersey.

As he closed the gate behind him, he heard the crunch of a spade in dirt. He stood motionless, his ear cocked. Had Mrs. Kinchman returned, he wondered. Was the insufferable woman lying in wait to take another shot at him? The morning after he'd dismissed her, he'd searched diligently through the garden looking for the derringer he'd removed from her person. He hadn't found it and strongly suspected she'd sneaked back and retrieved it.

Quietly, he made his way along the mulched side of the gravel path. The noise came from the back of the garden, in the patch where his aunt had cultivated herbs.

He stopped short. "Chloe?"

The child dropped her spade and looked up from the hole she'd been excavating. As she stared at him, the smudged pools of her eyes widened with guilt and fear. She wore only her shift. A streak of dirt ran the length of her forearm to her wrist, and her hair hung around her thin shoulders in unkempt ringlets.

"What are you doing out here at this hour?"

Visibly trembling, her dilated eyes fixed on him, she stepped backward. Oliver realized he must look like the bogeyman to her, appearing out of the misty light dressed in black from head to toe. He rearranged his expression and softened his voice.

"Chloe, don't be afraid. I was out on a little morning errand. That's why I'm dressed so oddly. Now tell me, what are you doing digging in the garden so early in the morning? Couldn't you sleep?"

She dropped her gaze to her muddy feet. He had been dimly aware of an object lying on the ground next to them. Now, he looked more closely and saw a narrow white box that he recognized. He lifted the lid. Still encased in tissue paper, Mrs. Pringle lay inside.

"Are you planning to bury your new doll? Do you dislike her that much?"

"I have to bury her. She died."

"I see." Oliver studied the doll. It did not appear to be damaged in any way. It's hair still spilled in golden profusion about its china face. Its lace skirts were still arranged in neat folds around its leather shoes. Carefully, he replaced the lid on the box. "I'm sorry to hear that Mrs. Pringle is gone. I know she's been ill. Did she die of her illness?"

Chloe shook her head. "She killed herself. She found a gun and shot herself."

"She did? She must have been very unhappy."

"She was."

He picked up the spade.

"Papa, what are you doing?"

"Making the hole deeper. How's that? Deep enough?"

Chloe nodded. Oliver placed the box in the hole, then handed her the spade. She filled the hole and patted the dirt smooth over the small mound.

"Do you think we should say a few words?"

Chloe nodded shyly.

"She's your doll. What would you like to say?"

Chloe bowed her head. "Please God, take Mrs. Pringle to heaven and make her happy." The little girl's voice began to shake. "She was too beautiful to be on earth. Make her happy in heaven." A tear trickled down her cheek.

Impulsively, he gathered her into his arms and pressed her against his chest. With one hand, he cupped the back of her head while his other stroked her back. "Chloe, Chloe, you're crying. Why? Why are you crying for Mrs. Pringle? I thought you didn't like her."

"She looked like Mama!" Chloe gasped between shudders. "Mama's never coming back, either."

He hugged Chloe closer. After a while he carried her inside the darkened house and up the stairs. They passed by Mrs. Milawney's room and the housekeeper stuck her head out. Oliver waved her away, and after raising her eyebrows she withdrew and shut her door.

Oliver laid Chloe down on her bed. She had stopped crying, but she looked exhausted. He sat stroking her hair while he watched her eyelids sink. As he pulled the mosquito netting around her, he realized that it truly no longer mattered whether this child was his blood or not. She was his daughter.

Morning light crept through the window. He reached into his shirt and took out the files hidden there. They were folded round the wad of loose papers he'd scooped up off the top of Sanders' desk on his first disastrous visit to the man's office.

Carrying them to the window, he glanced through the ragtag collection of scribbled notes and bills. A rough ink drawing caught his attention. It was a map of the area around City Hall with several x's and red dots scattered over it. At the top of the map someone had scribbled in a date and time. Wednesday, June 22nd at eleven o'clock.

CHAPTER THIRTY-TWO

Mrs. Milawney tapped on Oliver's open library door. The young lady, the one as used to work for you, left this, sir."

Groggily, he looked up from the files he'd been studying for the past two hours. Wordlessly, he accepted the letter and slit it open. It was from Hannah Kinchman.

Dear Mr. Redcastle, I hope this finds you in good health. Though you have seen fit to dismiss me from your employ, I feel that in good conscience I should make a final report before I leave Baltimore to try and find another way to help my wronged brother. As you requested, I established a relationship with Beacher Penrose. You were right to think there might be a connection between Mr. Penrose's deceased wife and Enoch Rubman. I have discovered from more than one source that Flora Penrose and Mr. Rubman were lovers. What is more, it seems Flora contracted syphilis from Rubman shortly before she took her own life. However, I do not believe there is any reason to think that Penrose could have been involved in Rubman's death as he is simply not a killer. Sincerely, Hannah Kinchman.

Oliver crumpled her letter and tossed it across the room. How did she know that Penrose wasn't a killer? Woman's intuition? Obviously, she'd become infatuated with Penrose and was incapable of making a clearheaded judgment. He picked up the letter and reread it. Then he put on his jacket. Outside in the hall he ran into Mrs. Milawney dusting the mirror.

"Is Chloe still abed?"

"She is, indeed sir, like a drowsy little angel. Shall I wake her?"

"No, let her sleep."

Mrs. Milawney smiled. "The best way to have the world beat a path to your door is to try and take a nap, don't you know. I won't let anyone disturb the poor little mite, sir. You can be sure of that."

After stopping in the kitchen for some cold ham and lemonade, Oliver flagged a hack. It took him to the telegraph office where he sent a message to William Pinkerton regarding Hannah's brother. See that Lewis gets out of jail. If Johnny Lewis came gunning for him after he was released, he'd have to get in line.

Oliver proceeded to the Rinehart School of Advanced Sculpture. A prune-faced woman pounding furiously on a typewriting machine directed him to the second floor.

"I'd knock first if I were you. When Mr. Penrose is working with a model he doesn't care to be disturbed."

"Is he working with a model now?"

"Not that I'm aware, but I know he's up there. He came in early this morning and hasn't left."

Oliver thanked her and climbed the marble steps. Penrose's studio was at the end of a wide, dimly lit corridor smelling of wax and turpentine. Though his door was closed, several others along the way hung open. Oliver spied students working at easels or hunks of clay and rough stone. The place seemed to hum like a hive of highly individualistic bees.

He knocked at Penrose's door several times, but got no response. One of the students, a paint-daubed youth with a scraggly beard, peered out of a nearby studio.

"Is Mr. Penrose here?" Oliver asked.

"So far as I know. I never saw him leave."

Oliver could not deny the feeling of urgency creeping over him. He knocked one more time, then went back downstairs and demanded that the typist find a way to unlock Penrose's door.

"That's quite impossible, I assure you."

"You mean you don't own a master key? What if Penrose should lose his keys? What then?"

She glared. "Well, I do have a master key. But I'd never use it on Mr. Penrose's door! He'd be furious."

"If he's had an accident in his studio and is sick or unconscious, he'll be even more furious if we don't go to his aid." Oliver dragged her and her keys up the stairs. She protested at every step.

"Perhaps he's just fallen asleep. Or perhaps he left and I never saw him go."

"We'll soon find out." Oliver wrestled the keys from her grip and unlocked the door. Aghast, he and the typist stared into the sunlit room. He caught her just as she was sliding to the floor in a dead faint.

At the commotion, several people emerged from the next studio. Oliver addressed an older man who looked like an instructor. "Please take this lady where she can lie down. Beacher Penrose has hung himself in his studio. If you would be so good as to direct one of your students to contact the police, I will stay with the body."

The building exploded into shocked mayhem. Students ran in and out of rooms, crying out the news. Their horrified voices bounced off the ceiling. Some students crowded around trying to get a look into Penrose's studio.

Oliver shooed them off and shut the artist's door. With his hands behind his back, he contemplated the dead man. Apparently, Penrose had stood on a chair and thrown a rope over a hook in the ceiling. He must have screwed it in himself for this express purpose.

A hanged man is not a pretty sight. Penrose's formerly comely face was now twisted and discolored. In contrast, picked out by the strong light streaming through the window behind him, his raven curls seemed to glisten with a life of their own. His long, sensitive hands, forever stilled, dangled pathetically at his sides.

A paper lay next to the chair he'd kicked over in his death throes. On it he had written, "Oh God, if you exist, have compassion on me and my selfish weakness."

As Oliver read the words, a deep sadness deadened his sense of shock. He had come here hoping to learn more from Penrose about Enoch Rubman's death. Now it was too late for that. He stared at the dead man's dangling feet. They must have danced and jerked during his death throes. Perhaps at that point he'd regretted ending his own life. The shadows of other hanged men seemed to whisper behind him. The Lewis brothers hadn't had any choice in how they'd died.

After one last glance at the artist, he looked around the room. A lifesize carving near the window attracted him. With growing admiration, he studied it. Clearly, Penrose had been a very gifted sculptor. The statue, which was oddly shaped and reached only to Oliver's knee, was of a naked crouching woman. She'd tucked her knees and slender calves up under her belly. Her long hair fell over her face and outstretched arms.

The lovely creature had been carved with such perfection that Oliver bent to touch it. Her curved back and rounded flank felt like cold silk against his palm. He was almost surprised that the stone flesh was not as warm and soft as it looked.

Recognition dawned and his hand shot back. This was Hannah Kinchman. She had posed for this statue. Jamming his hands into his pockets, he walked around the thing. The woman had stripped herself naked for Penrose's eyes. What other female did he know who would do such a thing? Marietta, he thought. Actresses, they were a breed apart.

He turned away and studied the other objects in the room. The wall opposite Penrose was stacked with paintings. A portrait of a naked, dark-haired woman with a beautiful face but a rather boyish looking body had been turned forward. The artist would have been looking at it as he strangled to death. Guessing that the portrait must be of Penrose's wife, Flora, Oliver spent several minutes studying it.

After a time, he began leafing through the other paintings

shoved up against the wall in untidy piles. He came upon a ser-ies of pen and ink drawings capturing street life in Baltimore. Penrose had evidently been in the habit of strolling about with a sketching pad. Oliver examined the works with interest and respect. He almost smiled as he flipped through a collection showing vendors haggling comically with patrons at the fish market. On the next drawing, his hand paused and he stared in shock.

He became aware of excited voices just outside the room. Seconds before a uniformed policeman flung the door open, he'd folded the drawing and pocketed it.

CHAPTER THIRTY-THREE

Mrs. Battaile informed Oliver, "You're too late. Mrs. Kinchman packed her bags and left yesterday. She didn't leave a forwarding address."

He walked out of the boarding establishment and crossed the street behind a team of horses hauling watermelons. It was now late in the afternoon. After finally disentangling himself from the ruckus at Penrose's studio, he'd gone to Mrs. Battaile's thinking he should inform Hannah of the artist's suicide. He also wished to let her know that he'd made arrangements for her brother's release from jail. Now, that would have to wait.

He flagged a hack and directed it to Felicia Rubman's house. As he sat back on the horsehair seat, he glanced over his shoulder and caught sight of Cyrus Roe slipping out from an alleyway and summoning his own hack. Was that young nincompoop playing amateur detective again? Grimacing, Oliver put his fingertips together and reviewed the status of this ever more frustrating case.

Who had sabotaged John D. Rockefeller's private railroad car and why? All three of the men killed in the so-called accident had known how to make enemies. Magruder and Nutwell had committed atrocities during the war, and now the city was teeming with veterans who might have seized upon the encampment as an opportunity for revenge.

Though Enoch Rubman's war record appeared honorable enough, he was no angel. Beacher Penrose had had plenty of reason to want the man dead. Rubman had seduced Penrose's wife, possibly given her syphilis and, presumably, been at least the partial cause of her suicide. Penrose's note had indicated that he'd hung himself because of a guilty conscience. Guilty about what? Had he sabotaged that railroad car to avenge his wife's death?

Oliver withdrew Penrose's folded sketch from his jacket and smoothed it on his knee. Could his first impression of what it contained be wrong?

No. Whatever else he may have been, Beacher Penrose was a gifted portrait artist who could capture character with a few swift but sure lines. The drawing Oliver had taken from his studio showed three men having what looked like a furtive discussion in a dark corner of a gambling hall. The conspirators were Marshal Rackley, Edson Bailey and Oliver's cousin, Griff Singleton--and Griff wasn't wearing his dark glasses.

"Damn you all to hell!" A dark-haired, strongly built man in a derby hat and canvas box coat bolted out of the Rubman front door and brushed rudely past Oliver. He stared after the fellow, then turned and looked quizzically at Mary McClarty, the Rubman's maid. She stood squarely in the doorway as if she were guarding a drawbridge.

"Who was that gentleman?"

"That was Mr. Dexter Rubman, sir, Mr. Enoch Rubman's brother. He's just been having a visit with Mrs. Rubman."

"Not a happy one, apparently."

"That's as may be. If you're here to see my mistress yourself, sir, I have to tell you she's not receiving. She miscarried last week and has been confined to her bed. I should never have let Mr. Rubman's brother visit with her, because he's upset her something terrible."

"I see. How unfortunate. I had hoped to ask Mrs. Rubman a few questions."

"Not today, sir."

Mary started to shut the door, but he prevented her by using his foot as a doorstop. "If I can't talk to your mistress, then perhaps you'll answer my questions."

"This is a busy household, and I've got work to do."

He plucked a bill from his pocket and waved it under her nose. "Can I buy fifteen minutes of your time?"

Mary looked behind her, then shut the door and motioned him around to the shady side of the house where a hedge of lilacs formed a natural screen.

As he followed her, Oliver glanced about to see if Cyrus Roe was anywhere in the neighborhood. If he was, he was keeping himself well hidden.

"Keep your voice low," Mary whispered. "Now what is it you're after? Why are you pokin' into my poor, sick mistress's business?"

"I'm trying to get the truth of her husband's death."

"The truth of it? You mean you think it wasn't an accident?" Mary's brows shot up.

"I don't know, but I'd like to find out. Now, tell me, what was Dexter Rubman doing here this afternoon?"

"He said it was to condole with her, but really it was to try and talk my lady into turning over her husband's war diary and all his other war papers. I heard them arguing."

"Why were they arguing?"

"She wouldn't do it. Wants to keep all her husbands things to pass onto his sons. Says it's her sacred duty."

"Does she know what this diary contains?"

"Her?" Mary snorted. "Not likely. All she reads is romantic novels and her Bible. Now, can I have my money?"

She tried to snatch at the bill, but Oliver held it out of her reach. "One more question. What do you know about your master's love affair with Flora Penrose?"

Mary's eyes widened. "How'd you hear about that?"

"Earlier today Beacher Penrose hanged himself. He left a suicide note."

The note hadn't mentioned Enoch Rubman's affair with Flora, but Oliver's tone implied that it had. Mary looked truly shocked. "Jesus, Joseph and Mary! I hope this isn't going to get back to my mistress. It will kill her, poor little thing! She's as innocent as a baby bird and twice as blind and trusting."

"You possess a very sharp pair of eyes. What did you see going on between Rubman and Penrose's wife?"

"Not much. He gave her his blather and took her to bed, I dare say. Enoch liked the women, but never stuck to one for long. When he moved on she took and hung herself, poor silly fool." She reached for her money and Oliver let her have it.

"If I gave you another five, would you get me that diary to read?"

"Steal it for you?" Mary shook her head. "I'm no thief!" She danced away.

After the door banged closed behind her, Oliver gazed at the windows of the house. He pitied Felicia Rubman. Was it possible that she'd miscarried because her promiscuous husband had infected her with syphilis? If so, Enoch Rubman had deserved his fiery end. But who had engineered it? And where was Rubman's diary kept?

He made his way back to the street where, fortunately, his hack still waited. There was no sign of Roe, though Oliver was sure the eager-beaver investigator had followed him. Maybe he'd got tired of acting like a sleuth in a dime novel and gone home.

Back in Baltimore, Oliver told his driver to let him off at Daly's saloon on St. Paul Street. It wasn't just that he needed a drink, which he did. As the hack had rolled past the saloon, he'd caught sight of a piebald horse tied to a hitching post. He'd noticed that same horse in front of the Rubman house, and Dexter Rubman had been its rider.

Inside the saloon, which also rented rooms on its second floor, he spotted Dexter brooding over a mug of ale. Oliver took a stool next to his.

"Another pint for this gentleman and one like it for myself."

Dexter turned his head. "Who the hell are you?"

"A friend. I happen to be acquainted with Mrs. Felicia Rubman. You're her brother-in-law, are you not?"

"What's it to you?"

"Since you're new in town, I thought I might offer you a drink and some conversation."

"If there's anything I won't tolerate, it's a busybody. I don't care to talk to you, and I don't want your damned drink!" Rubman downed his ale and shoved the empty glass at the barman. "Put this on my tab." He stalked to the back of the bar and disappeared up the staircase that led to the second floor.

"Nice fella'" the bartender commented.

"Is he always that sociable?"

"Took a room yesterday and hasn't said more than he needs to. We're used to surly fellas around here. All right with me so long as he pays his bill. Now, what about you, Mister? Drinks are a quarter a piece and you've ordered two, so that'll be half a dollar."

CHAPTER
THIRTY-FOUR

"Our losses this day were fearsome, and our men were exhausted and sorely in need of succor. Necessity forced me to commandeer the Rubman brothers and two other men I discovered hanging back from the fighting. Since the four had proved worse than useless in combat, I sent them out on a provisioning mission to scour the local populace and gather what they may discover to keep our men supplied with food, clothing and horses."

Oliver read and re-read the lines until the faded, spidery script seemed to dance in the gaslight. The report had been set down by the captain in Rubman's company at Antietam.

Oliver had spent that evening combing through the war files of Magruder, Rubman and Nutwell. They'd all had scattered military careers, moving from one company to another as they served out their three-year terms. What was the point of intersection, he'd kept asking himself. What had made them friendly enough to journey to the encampment together in that railroad car? Was it just chance, or did some single incident bind them to one another?

This report from the bloody massacre at Antietam where they'd all served suggested interesting possibilities. Rubman's brother, Dexter, had been part of a foursome licensed to steal from the local farmers in the name of military necessity. Dexter was the only one left who could tell that tale. Unless, of course, it was recorded in Enoch Rubman's diary. Had those two other men who'd made up the foraging party been Magruder and Nutwell?

Oliver glanced at the clock. It was after midnight. Hours ago Chloe and Mrs. Milawney had gone to bed. He wished he could do the same. Instead, he rolled down his shirtsleeves, donned his jacket and left the house.

A hack easily took him back to Daly's. But Dexter Rubman was not to be found. The barkeep told Oliver he'd left an hour and a half earlier and hadn't returned.

"Got no idea where he went and don't care, neither."

Oliver walked out of the saloon with his brow furrowed. Like the other veterans jamming the town, Dexter might be carousing in waterfront bars or making a fool of himself at a house of ill repute. But Oliver thought not.

On a hunch, he went to the livery stable in the alley behind Daly's. There the stable boy, a dimwitted individual with hair that looked exactly like the straw he pitched for his horses, said that a man answering Dexter Rubman's description had changed his piebald for a fresh bay and ridden out "not too long ago."

"Busy night 'round here," he added.

"What do you mean?"

"'Nother fella' came in just after the first and hired hisself a horse, and now you'll be wantin' one, too."

Oliver nodded and dug inside his pocket for a dollar. A few minutes later he was mounted on a swaybacked sorrel gelding and headed north toward the Rubman house.

The day's humidity lingered in the night air like a whore's sticky kiss. A thick layer of cloud swathed the gibbous moon. Once past the light of the city, the road and surrounding fields seemed smothered in a bath of ink. Farmers and tradesmen kept the route he'd taken well traveled by day, but it was lonely now. The trees furring the edges of the lane swallowed up the clop of the gelding's hooves. Off to the left a hunting owl hooted.

It all felt familiar. So often in his career as a lawman he had ridden out at night on dubious errands. Before that, when he'd been a sixteen-year-old sharpshooter, the night had been his special ally. There was usually no killing at night, and if he'd hidden himself well enough, he was safe until morning.

It had been night when his commanding officer had brought him the telegram about Quantrill's raid and the murder of his family. He had read and reread it with disbelief. Despite the war death around him, he hadn't been able to imagine his mother and father and his brothers dead. Kansas seemed like another world, another time. How could this plague of death have found its way there?

He had run away and let the darkness hide him. Not until the next morning, when the well of his tears had dried and the only thing left was hatred and a burning desire for revenge, had he returned to his company. Every time he took aim at a target, the blank faces of the men who had murdered his mother rose up before him.

As Oliver urged his sorry animal to quicken its pace, he speculated about what Dexter Rubman might be doing. It was likely that Dexter had learned where Felicia kept the diary. Even now, he might be spiriting it away. Oliver hoped the man wasn't such a clumsy burglar that he'd be caught before he could intercept him and acquire the diary for himself. It might be the key he needed to make sense of this case.

He pulled up. If he'd guessed right and Dexter really was pilfering the diary, it wouldn't do to blunder into him as he returned from Felicia's house. It would be better to waylay him at some promising spot.

He was just looking around for such a vantage point when his gelding's ears pricked up. Another horse whickered in the distance. He guided his horse to the side of the road and waited. The stranger animal whickered again, this time closer at hand. An iron-shod hoof rang against a stone. Oliver drew his gun and rode forward, hoping to cut off Dexter Rubman's flight back to town. Instead, he intercepted a riderless horse. It's empty saddle was still warm.

Oliver tied the animal's reins to a branch, then remounted his sorrel and backtracked slowly. Cursing the cloud cover, which made it quite possible that he might pass a fallen body lying at the side of the road without even seeing it, he squinted into the darkness.

About a quarter of a mile from Felicia Rubman's house, he heard another horse stamp its feet and snuffle. This time the noise came from a field to his right. He turned off the lane and rode through a stand of corn, following the faint sounds. It might be a wild goose chase. Farmers commonly left their stock out on warm summer nights. But the prickle at the back of his neck urged him forward.

When the clouds parted enough to cast a grayish sheen, he saw the outline of a riding horse munching fallen apples next to a tree. Dismounting, he looped his reins over one of the tree's lower branches and approached the animal.

A shaft of white moonlight fell on the trampled ground, picking out a large, twisted black lump. The lump turned out to be Dexter Rubman. Though his body was still warm, he was quite dead. When Oliver touched his head, his fingers came back covered with sticky blood. Dexter could, of course, have fallen off his horse. Oliver figured not. He looked around until he discovered a stout wooden club lying about fifteen feet from Dexter's body. It, too, was gluey with blood. Somebody had used it to beat the man's head in.

CHAPTER THIRTY-FIVE

"**Y**ou step into sinkholes wherever you march, don't you Redcastle?"

Marshal Rackley's ruined voice crashed out over the soft morning air. "Josiah Jackson," he went on, naming the captain of the Northern district, "tells me you turned up another corpse last night. That's two in less than twenty-four hours. Keep it up and you'll get mighty popular with the local undertakers."

"But not so popular with you, I'd guess." It had been a long night, and a disappointing one. Though Oliver had searched high and low before reporting Dexter's murder, he hadn't found Enoch Rubman's diary. Either Dexter had been killed before he got to the Rubman house, or his murderer had taken the diary with him. Maybe he had even killed Dexter for the diary.

"I'm not fond of trouble, nor of folks who bring it," Rackley bristled. Behind him, pheasants still squawked in the dewy hedgerows bordering the Singleton mansion.

At this early hour, Oliver was surprised to run into the deputy marshal leaving Zephyrus. What did he and Griff have to talk about that required so many visits? Aloud, he said, "The horse I found abandoned on the York Road was from the same stable where Dexter and I rented our mounts. I'll wager that once Jackson gets a description from the stable boy, he'll have the killer."

"The stable boy happens to be feebleminded. A description from him wouldn't amount to a cup of cat piss. Speaking of using the brains God gave you, have you decided about that little investment opportunity we discussed?" Rackley tapped a buggy whip against his fat palm.

"I'll let you know in a couple of days."

"Shit or get off the chamber pot! You've got two hours to put down your money, Redcastle. Opportunities like ours don't grow on trees. My town can be unhealthy if you haven't bothered to make the right friends."

He hoisted his bulk into his pony cart, snapped his whip smartly on his horse's rump and drove off. When he was out of sight, Oliver walked up to Zephyrus' massive front door. A servant let him in. There was no sign of Laura, which was a blessing. He wanted to see Griff alone.

The servant led him to a library. Dressed in his customary white suit and dark glasses, Griff waited in a leather wing chair, his legs crossed. His ankles looked skeletal, like a much older man's.

"Another delightful surprise." Griff's tone suggested it was no such thing. "I presume this isn't a purely social visit, cousin. To what do I owe the pleasure?"

"I'm not here to take up your time, Griff, so I'll get right to the point."

"Suit yourself, cousin, though I assure you it's not in the least necessary to preserve me from the tedium of idle minutes. I have all the time in the world. No pressing business calls me-- or ever will, most likely."

Oliver withdrew Beacher Penrose's sketch from his jacket. "Do you recognize this?" He laid the sketch in Griff's lap.

It fluttered to the floor untouched. "Ollie," Griff said with a light protesting laugh, "how can I recognize a piece of paper if I can't properly see it?"

Oliver snatched the glasses from his cousin's face and tossed them onto the desk. Griff jerked his hands up in protest and half stood. Then he sank back down. His eyes, fixed on Oliver, looked perfectly focused. "You've no right to invade my privacy in this damned crude manner! Give me back my glasses."

"Not until you tell me the truth. You can see as well as I can."

"Oh, I doubt that. You always did have eagle eyes, didn't you? That's what made you such an amazing shot. Even when we were striplings you could take all the prizes at the shooting galleries and make me look a fool."

"When did you regain your sight? How long have you been hiding behind dark glasses not needing them?"

Griff's face twisted. "All right, if you must know, two weeks after I escaped Point Lookout I could see almost as well as I ever did."

"Then why, for God's sake, why have you been pretending to be half blind all these years?"

"You wouldn't understand."

"Try me."

"I don't have much choice about that, do I? You're not going to leave me in peace until you've dragged it all out. Very well, if you must know, at first it was because I was afraid that Grandfather would insist I go back and fight. He would say the family honor demanded it, you know."

"You were afraid of fighting?"

"You can't comprehend that, can you Ollie? You've never been afraid of anything, have you?"

It was so far from the truth that he laughed. "During the war, I was scared shitless the whole time I served. The only thing that kept me going was my hate. I saw Quantrill's face on top of every Reb uniform."

"Maybe that's the difference between us. I didn't hate the Federals. After all, you were one of them and I always did like you even though I was jealous."

"Jealous of me?"

"Because of Laura. Laura had a soft spot for you. After Point Lookout, I knew I couldn't go back to being a soldier. If I did, I would surely wind up rotting just like all those other fellas in the peach orchard." Griff shivered. "Then there was Laura. She wouldn't have taken me if she'd known I could see again but didn't want to fight. She was determined I had to be a hero, so I catered to her whim. She married me out of pity, you know."

"That's not true. Laura loves you."

"You think so?" Griff made a derisive noise. "She loved me before the war. After it was over and Grandfather died, she loved the life I could give her here at Zephyrus. But love me? I couldn't do otherwise than go on pretending to be half blind. If I'd let her know I could see, she would have guessed I'd been lying all along. Everyone would have guessed. I would have been disgraced."

Oliver was stunned. In pretending to be an invalid all these years, Griff had turned himself into one. His body had become weak and shrunken and so had his character. All because of a misguided notion of honor and a desire to bind a woman to him.

Oliver picked up the sketch and jammed it at his cousin's face. "That is you, isn't it? You're in cahoots with Rackley and his crew of crooked investors."

Griff turned his head. "My private dealings are no business of yours."

"If your honor is so damned sacred, why are you involved in this shady scheme of Rackley's? You must know he and Bailey are trying to coax me into joining their cabal, yet you said nothing. You didn't want me to know you were in with them. Why? Because you know very well that it's not a straight deal?"

"There's nothing illegitimate about a dredging company."

"Even one depending on bribes to take advantage of a piece of pork barrel legislation that hasn't been signed into law yet?"

"The Rivers and Harbors Act will be passed this year. Everyone says so."

"It's common knowledge that President Arthur plans to veto the measure if it is passed. What's supposed to happen at eleven o'clock?"

Griff went white. "What?"

"That's when Arthur and most of his Cabinet is coming into town for the encampment." Oliver took out the doctored map of the streets surrounding City Hall. "I found this among your partner Sanders' paper. It's some kind of a plot. At first I couldn't figure what that X was supposed to be." Oliver pointed at the mark on the map. "But I've been a sniper myself, so now I've got it figured. The x marks the best spot to get a clear line of sight on City Hall where the President's party will review the parade. It's the Holiday Street theater, isn't it? If a man like Gloger wanted to get off a shot at Arthur, that's where he'd station himself."

Griff's stricken silence told the story. Oliver seized his cousin's collar and half lifted him out of his chair. His body felt surprisingly light, as if it were made of balsa.

"Good God, I'm right, aren't I? You and your crooked cronies are planning to assassinate Chester Arthur today."

CHAPTER THIRTY-SIX

The President, along with Attorney General Brewster, Postmaster General Howe, and Secretary of War Lincoln, had left Washington at ten that morning in a private car provided by John W. Garrett. Mayor Whyte, Garrett and others would escort the President's party to City Hall. There he would review a parade composed of two divisions. The first would be made up of regulars from Fort McHenry, Maryland, Virginia and the District of Columbia. The second would comprise Union Veterans.

Most stores and all the public buildings and banks closed for the festivities. A cloudless sky hung over Camden Yards where the President's train was due to arrive at eleven o'clock. From it the hot summer sun shone on women dressed in flag-draped skirts and children sporting red and white striped caps.

The buzz of movement spilled out onto Pratt and Howard streets. People waving flags and carrying noisemakers craned their necks to be among the first to see the President's train arrive. Behind the dull roar of their cheers and laughter, a band played popular tunes.

Harry Barnett should have arrived in advance of the President's party and might be supervising security at the train station. Hoping to warn him of the plot he'd uncovered, Oliver pushed through the gathering.

"Ho there, Redcastle, just the man I wanted to see."

Josiah Jackson, the Northern Distric police official handling the Dexter Rubman murder, shouldered aside a group of school children.

Oliver considered telling Jackson about the assassination plot afoot. But Jackson was under Rackley's thumb, and might be involved himself. Oliver asked, "Have you caught Dexter Rubman's murderer yet?"

"Not yet. But you had the right notion about that horse you found on the York Road. Sure enough, it belonged to the same outfit where Rubman rented his nag."

"Did the stableboy identify the man who rented it?"

"I wouldn't say he identified anybody," Jackson shouted above the gabble of a large family group pressing to get closer to the tracks. "He gave me a description, for what it's worth." Jackson leaned forward and whispered the description into Oliver's ear.

His eyebrows shot up. Jackson had described a personage who resembled Cyrus Roe. Oliver opened his mouth to speak, but the blast of a shrill whistle drowned his words. President Arthur's train was pulling in.

"Is Mr. Redcastle in?"

"No, Miss Kinchman, and I'm in such a dither!"

"What's wrong?" Hannah looked closely at Mrs. Milawney. The woman appeared flushed and breathless. Her reddened eyes glistened with tears.

"Come in. No reason to stand on the stoop so the neighbors can tattle about our business. Lord knows the old biddies have little enough to occupy their minds."

Hannah followed the housekeeper inside. She'd come to thank Oliver for his intercession on her brother's behalf and to attend Beacher Penrose's funeral. The news of his suicide had overwhelmed her with guilt. He'd already been staggering under the burden of his own self-blame. Had her angry words been the last straw?

"Oh the morning I've had," Mrs. Milawney moaned. "It's set my hair on end. My niece, Eva, has just sent me some terrible news about my grand nephew, Jimmy!"

"Has something happened to him?"

"Lordy, his mama is out in the fields for the summer with all her kiddies. She's breaking her back picking strawberries for the cannery. Wouldn't you know it, Jimmy, the scamp, goes and falls out of a tree and breaks his leg." Mrs. Milawney wrang her plump hands.

"Eva sends word asking me to help her take care of him. Lord knows his drunken no-good father won't be any earthly use. He's one of those men who started at the bottom and stayed there. But I've got Chloe to see to and no money in the house for a hack to get to the farm."

"I've got money." Hannah dug into her bag. "You should go see to your nephew immediately."

"But there's Chloe."

"I'll stay with her and explain to Mr. Redcastle when he comes back."

Half an hour later, Hannah and Chloe sat under the shade of the maple tree in the garden, playing at paper dolls. Chloe had shown Hannah Mrs. Pringle's grave and they'd picked roses to place on it.

"Do you think Mrs. Pringle might be feeling better now that she's had a rest?" Hannah asked.

"Oh no. She shot herself and died. When you're dead you never feel better."

"But perhaps she didn't really die. Dolls are different from people, you know."

Chloe scuffed the toe of her shoe against the small mound of dirt. "My papa gave me Mrs. Pringle when my mama died. Mrs. Pringle is like my mama. My mama's never coming back, and neither is Mrs. Pringle."

Hannah took Chloe's hand. "Your mama was an actress and so am I. It's a hard life. She didn't want to get sick and die. She didn't want to leave the ones she loved behind. Sometimes things happen that can't be controlled."

Chloe raised solemn eyes. "Did you ever have to leave your little girl behind?"

"I was never lucky enough to have my own little girl. I never had a papa who loved me, either. He died before I knew him and my mama was too tired and sick to spend much time with me. You've got a papa who loves you very much. I think he gave you Mrs. Pringle to show you his love. Why don't you dig her up? If she's like your mama she's an actress and actresses just pretend to shoot themselves. I bet anything that she's tired of being buried."

A sharp knock rattled the tall wood gate at the other end of the garden. Brushing leaves from her skirts, Hannah hurried down the path and Chloe followed. They arrived at the other side of the maple in time to see a woman's pale face appear around the open gate.

She exclaimed, "I'm sorry to intrude, but I've been knocking and knocking on the front door. I heard voices behind this gate. Mr. Redcastle told me to call if I should need help. Are you his wife?"

Hannah came forward. "I'm his associate and this is his daughter, Chloe. If you'll tell me your errand, perhaps I can help." She'd recognized Felicia Rubman, whom she'd seen from a distance while she'd cultivated a friendship with Mary McClarty. What was Enoch Rubman's widow doing here looking so ill?

Felicia tottered through the gate clutching a box. Hannah guided her to a bench in the maple's shade. Settling on it with a grateful sigh, the pale young woman placed her box on her lap and untied her bonnet strings. She was no longer huge with child. Indeed, her black dress hung on her small frame.

Freed of her veil and bonnet, Felicia's hair clustered around her perspiring face in damp spit curls. Her high-necked black mourning covered her down to her toes, but Hannah perceived stains from perspiration under its tight sleeves.

"You shouldn't be out in this heat," Hannah said solicitously. "I can see that you haven't been well."

"No, no I haven't." Felicia's eyes filled with tears. "The fates have been most cruel. I've lost my husband, and now I've lost my dear little baby, too."

"My dear lady, you should be home in your bed."

"Oh, I know, and the streets are so crowded. I'm far too ill to be here. But something so dreadful has happened. I had to consult Mr. Redcastle."

"What has upset you?"

Felicia's hands fluttered above her lap like distraught moths. "How can I explain? I thought Mr. Redcastle might understand, but he isn't here. It has to do with my dear husband's private papers."

Chloe tugged at Hannah's skirt to gain attention. "I'm going to go dig up Mrs. Pringle and see if she's alive."

"You do that, sweetheart." At Felicia's startled look, Hannah explained about the doll. "You mentioned your husband's private papers?"

"His war letters and diaries. Yesterday my brother-in-law came to see me about them. The man was never a proper brother to Enoch. Why, he didn't even attend our wedding. The one time he did visit, just after our son was born, he argued with my husband dreadfully."

"What did he want when he came to see you?"

"Enoch's letters and diaries. Of course, I refused. Those precious mementos will go to my eldest son when he's of age. When I told Dexter of my decision, he shouted all sorts of terrible threats. He said. . ." a fresh tear spilled down Felicia's cheek, "he said my husband was a criminal who deserved to die. Can you believe he would say such terrible things about my dear departed Enoch?"

"How shocking. Do you have any idea why he might have made that accusation?"

Felicia dabbed at her nose with a handkerchief. "Plainly, just for spite because I would not accede to his selfish and inconsiderate wishes. But then last night something so strange and terrible happened. A masked man broke into the house, held my maid Mary and myself at gunpoint and demanded that we give him Enoch's diaries."

"Was it your brother-in-law?"

"No, it was not. Despite his mask, I could see that easily. He was a much slighter man, and younger."

"Did you give him what he wanted?"

"I suppose I might have. I was so dreadfully frightened. But Mary, my maid, is a clever girl. She gave him only one of the diaries. He apparently didn't know there were three, you see. So I still have two left." Felicia tapped the box on her lap. "I've brought them to Mr. Redcastle in hopes he may be able to advise me about putting them in a safe place. But that's not the worst of it. Oh dear, no. This morning the police came and informed me that Dexter has been found murdered.

A scream from Chloe interrupted Felicia's words.

CHAPTER THIRTY-SEVEN

Banners, streamers and flags embellished City Hall. The streets and buildings surrounding it bore mottoes. "1776-1882," "One Country, One Constitution, One Destiny," "Welcome G.A.R.," "Welcome Veterans!"

Throngs of citizens, many of them encampment veterans in uniform, packed Holiday Street. Police pushed and shouted, trying to keep the route in front of City Hall open for the procession which had started forming on Broadway at nine o'clock and begun its march at 10.40. In the distance the rat-a-tat of oncoming drums could be heard.

President Arthur was still inside City Hall enjoying a reception with the mayor, John Garrett and other dignitaries. He would come out to the portico just before the procession passed.

Oliver shouldered his way through the multitude. All the world seemed gathered in this spot. He caught sight of Kitty Putnam with her girls, all of them patriotic in tight red, white and blue jackets and star-spangled bonnets. He'd already glimpsed John L. Sullivan looking jovial at the center of a group of his admirers.

Finally, he spotted Harry Barnett with a knot of other men near the President's empty coach. Oliver had to plunge through a line of police to get to him.

"Harry, I have to talk to you!"

"And I you. Garrett's been asking me what you've got on his railroad car crash. Anything I should get the wind up over?"

"There's this." Oliver thrust the diagram from Sanders' office under Harry's nose and told him what he knew of the plot to assassinate Arthur.

"Holy Jesus! You're sure about this?"

"I'm sure of nothing. I came to warn you, though that shouldn't be necessary if you've taken every precaution. I presume you've got snipers on all the roofs?"

"Of course."

"Then you're set. Now I've got to get back home. I've just learned something that worries me."

Harry seized Oliver's shoulder. "You can't drop this on me, then toddle off. I'm undermanned here."

"You're the one paid to guard the President, not me."

"You can't leave. Now that you're here, you've got to stay and help. You must see that. Here, let me take a closer look at this damned diagram." He scanned the tattered piece of paper and surveyed the swarming square.

Oliver looked across the street where, among other buildings, the Holiday Street Theater and the Voshell House faced City Hall, providing an excellent vantage point for a marksmen drawing a bead on Arthur.

"It could be any one of those buildings," Harry muttered, "but the theater looks most promising, wouldn't you say? McKinney is up there."

Hired by the Pinkertons shortly before Oliver put in his resignation, McKinney was a young fellow with a sure-shot reputation.

"Who else is with him?"

"He's alone. I told you, we're shorthanded."

"How much time did you spend getting the lay of that theater?" Oliver studied the theater's facade. It was a three-story building with a smaller garret story centered on the roof. Several windows would accommodate a shooter nicely.

"Not enough," Harry admitted. "Not as much as I would have if I'd known there was a plot afoot. McKinney's on the roof, but a man might slip in on the floor below and make use of one of those oculus windows without McKinnney being the wiser until it was too late." Harry chewed his bottom lip. "Go over and have a look, will you, Ollie? We can't have another President assassinated on our watch, not after Garfield and Lincoln."

Oliver scanned the crowd. Just to get through it and across the street to the theater would be a challenge

"Do it for old times sake," Harry cajoled. "You owe me, Ollie, you know you do. Besides, chances are this is all just a hoax."

Oliver hoped Harry was right. With a sigh, he agreed to help. Ten minutes later he'd managed to shove his way through the ever-thickening crowd. Fortunately, most of the people in it were in a festive mood. Even so, several had shaken their fists at him as he'd pushed past.

The theater, of course, had been locked up tight in front. Around back, he found a policeman guarding the rear entrance. Harry had written him a pass. The man stared at it suspiciously, then handed it back.

"I've got orders not to let anybody else through."

"Harry Barnett is in charge of the President's security and Barnett's the one who wrote this pass. You can see his official stamp right there."

"Maybe so, but city law officers such as myself are responsible for building security and Marshal Rackley gave me my orders not half an hour ago."

"Is Rackley inside?"

"Nobody's inside but the Pinkerton man guarding the roof, and things are going to stay that way!"

Instead of wasting time arguing, Oliver walked off. It would have been easy for Rackley to distract the guard's attention and slip someone into the theater without anyone being the wiser. Drifting over the hubbub of the crowd, the beat of drums and martial music signaled the advance of the procession. It was getting close. If President Arthur and his party weren't already outside City Hall, they soon would be.

Oliver circled the block, came up behind the policeman guarding the theater entrance and flattened him with the butt end of his Colt. As the man sagged into the doorway, Oliver forced the door open and dragged him inside. After checking his pulse and relieving him of his gun, brass knuckles and billy club, he left him on the floor and proceeded up a flight of ill-lighted stairs leading to the rear of the stage.

Quickly investigating a series of drops and flats onstage, he assured himself that the theater was empty. He cast a worried glance upward, then returned to the stairs and climbed to the second level. From there, he was able to look out over the many pipe battens holding up curtains and painted flats. To the left there was a railing with a narrow walkway. Up a level there was a similar platform. Above that a series of fly lines, grids, pulleys and counterweights spanned the area over the stage. A narrow ladder running up all three levels had been pinned to the wall. But it would take a monkey to climb it, Oliver thought, and already his knee was aching. He proceeded up the more conventional stairs.

They took him to the third level where a small, grimy window looked out on a surging mass of merrymakers. A final rickety wood staircase led to a platform above the grid. It was impossible to tell if anyone occupied the platform. Presumably McKinney was out on the roof. Gun in hand, Oliver began to ascend the steps. He cursed the inevitable squeaks and groans of the splintery wood under his feet. If someone were up there who shouldn't be, the noise would alert them.

On a landing halfway up, Oliver paused to rest his leg. As he massaged it, he peered out another slit window. Not four blocks away he saw the bobbing snake of blue that was the procession. Its sabers and bayonets flashed in the sunlight. The doors leading off City Hall's portico had been thrown open, though as yet no dignitaries had emerged.

He straightened and pushed on. As he neared the top, the hair on the back of his neck began to lift. He was a sitting duck for anyone who wanted to shoot down and pick him off. Gingerly, he mounted the few remaining steps. As his head came level with the platform surrounding the system of pulleys and counterweights, he saw McKinney's crumpled body.

A gun barrel was thrust hard into the back of his neck. "Nice of you to pay a visit," Marshal Rackley's voice rumbled. "Now when Gloger picks Arthur off, instead of pinning it on the Pinkerton, we can pin it on you. Can't we, Griff?"

"Stay where you are or I'll wring the kid's neck." Hannah stared at the young man pointing a revolver. His babyish face twisted with hate as he crushed Chloe against his body and flattened his hand over her mouth.

He'd climbed the back fence and surprised the child excavating Mrs. Pringle's grave. A pile of dirt and an abandoned spade lay next to the hole. Mrs. Pringle's box, the lid half off, was visible at the bottom.

Felicia Rubman shrieked, "It's him! It's the one in the mask. Oh God in heaven, he's followed me here!"

Hannah, who was desperately trying to make sense of all this, took her eyes off Chloe long enough to glance back at Felicia. She looked as if she were going to faint.

Hannah returned her attention to the intruder. "Who are you? What do you want?"

"I want that!" He jabbed his gun at Felicia's box. "And I mean to have it," he added, addressing her. "You won't fool me this time. The diary you gave me last night ran out before Antietam. I want to read what he had to say about Antietam. Hand over the box!"

Felicia shook her head. "Never! I'm keeping my precious husband's writings for his sons."

"Your sons would be happier not knowing what your precious husband did in the war."

"My Enoch was a hero."

"He was a damned rapist and murderer. He and his pals raped my sister and shot my brother like a dog."

"That can't be true!"

"Can't it? My brother, Nate, fought sesesh. When he got himself wounded at Dunker's church, he crawled home. Martha and me, we hid him in a cave. That's where your husband and his friends found us. Me, I was only four years old. I hid at the back of the cave and saw what they did. Later, I watched my sister die trying to birth the child that came from their sin. I swore someday I'd make them pay."

"You're insane!"

"I'm the angel of righteous retribution. It's been a long time coming, but those four Yankee devils have paid now, haven't they? I've seen to it. Give me the box. That diary will prove what they did. No jury will blame me once it knows the God's truth."

Felicia took a step backward. "How dare you say such things? You're mad!"

In an agony of apprehension, Hannah said, "Felicia, you must do as this man says. Otherwise, Chloe may be hurt."

"Never!" Felicia turned and made as if to totter away. Hannah dragged her back by her hair.

Felicia screamed and struggled, all the while still clutching her box. Her hair, loosened from its pins, hung in medusa-like ringlets around her face. "I will never, never accede to this foul fiend's wishes!" she hissed through clenched teeth.

Hannah threw her to the ground. The box rolled into Mrs. Pringle's open grave.

"Oh, oh!" Felicia lay in the dirt, sobbing. She drew her knees up to her chest. "Oh why, why, why is all this happening? Oh God, what have I done?"

"Leave her alone!" Chloe's captor shouted when Hannah touched Felicia's heaving shoulder. "Get the damned box and give it to me now! Otherwise, I'll kill the kid and you, too. I've got nothing to lose now, do you hear?"

Hannah crawled after the box. It had dislodged Mrs. Pringle. The doll's cardboard coffin lay on its side, the rest of its contents spilled. Hannah's eyes widened. She reached into the hole and her hand touched the derringer Oliver Redcastle had wrested from her earlier that week. Chloe must have found it and buried it with Mrs. Pringle.

CHAPTER THIRTY-EIGHT

Marshal Rackley confiscated Oliver's gun and forced him up onto the platform. "What are you going to do about this fella, Griff?"

"I suppose you'll have to kill him."

Rackley chuckled nastily. "You mean you will. No chance of you missing him this time around, not at this distance."

Ignoring Rackley, Oliver stared at Griff. Devoid of his glasses, and wearing the questionable disguise of a Union uniform a size too big for him, he looked shrunken and misplaced. The gun in his right hand dangled from his fingers, its business end perpendicular to the floor.

"It was you who shot me at Druid Hill Park. Why?"

"I followed Laura to the park that morning. I saw you sneaking a rendezvous with her. You came back to Baltimore to take my wife from me, didn't you?"

"Griff, for God's sake man, that's not. . .!"

Rackley prodded Oliver's kidney with the barrel of his gun. "Enough of this blather, Singleton. Gloger's already on the roof. Another few minutes and he'll have pulled the trigger. Now here's the way I see it. Instead of pinning the deed on McKinney, like we planned, we'll say Redcastle did it. He snuck in here, see, killed the Pinkerton and shot Arthur. Then I nabbed him trying to escape and blew his brains out."

"Charming," Oliver commented, "but you've left out one element. Why would I want to assassinate President Arthur?"

"To embarrass the Pinkertons. Wouldn't have quit them if

you didn't have a grudge. Most likely, they fired you."

Oliver had no chance to correct this misapprehension, as Rackley had returned his attention to Griff. "Now's the time to show you're a man. Blow your meddling cousin to kingdom come."

When Griff didn't move, Rackley let out an exasperated wheeze. "Dammit to hell, Singleton, I'm tired of doing all your dirty work. This time it's you who'll have blood on your hands. Shoot Redcastle!"

Oliver watched his cousin lift his weapon and point it. He had heard that a drowning man's past flashes before him. Now, a curious detachment came over him as scenes from his boyhood with Griff danced before his mind's eye. He saw the two of them in Bombick's gym, vying to swing the Indian clubs. He saw them sneaking away to buy candy and take in the oddities at Herzog's dime museum. Dimly he seemed to hear the music of the hurdy-gurdy mingled with their boyish laughter.

Through the haze of these ghostly images, he saw the barrel of Griff's gun waver and then shake. A bullet exploded from it. Oliver felt it sting the outside of his left thigh. He clutched at his belly, bent over double and howled as if in his death throes.

"That's the ticket!" Rackley maneuvered around Oliver's doubled over body and rushed up to Griff. "Shoot him again just to make sure."

"What the hell is going on down here?" A trap door in the roof opened and Gloger stuck his head through it. His jaw dropped when he saw Oliver crumpled below him.

Excitedly, Rackley explained the change in their plans but Gloger objected.

"Arthur isn't going to get shot with a Remington-Beals single shot."

"What does that matter?"

"Everyone knows that's what Redcastle would use for a sniper job."

"It's a minor detail. We'll say he used McKinney's gun to make it look as if McKinney did it."

"I'd still like to get my hands on that Remington-Beals. They're scarce as hen's teeth. With Redcastle out of the way, this would be a good time for his Beals to go missing."

"I don't give an outhouse fart for his gun!" Rackley exclaimed in exasperation.

Gloger's eyes narrowed. "But I do. It'd make me a lot happier about this job I'm doing for you if I could go home with that rifle."

Cursing, Rackley whirled on Griff. "Go to Redcastle's house and get hold of his rifle."

"How?"

"Dammit man, you're his cousin. He's only got a housekeeper and a kid living with him. They're probably not even at home."

"What will I do with it once I've got it? I won't be able to bring it back here. By then all hell will have broken loose."

"Just get your hands on it," Rackley hissed. "I'll take the business from there."

Griff rushed down the steps. A roar rose from the crowd outside, drowning out the tap of his feet on the wooden treads.

"Almost time," Gloger said. He pulled back out of sight and the trap door thudded closed.

As it cut out the light, Oliver rolled over, launched himself at Rackley's broad backside and sent him sprawling lengthwise. Half his thick torso slid over the narrow opening down which the ropes holding up the many drops and flats dangled.

"Holy hell!" he yelped. "You've been playing possum!" Puffing like steam engine, he began hauling himself back over the edge of the platform. Oliver kicked him and his other leg went over the edge. The man had tremendous strength in his thick shoulders and arms. Though half his weight hung free, he still held onto the platform.

Sweating like a turkey in an oven, he stared up at Oliver. "For God's sake, man, if I fall I'll break my back. Do you want that on your conscience?"

"Don't have much choice, do I?" Oliver answered. The roar

of the crowd outside was now almost deafening. At any moment Gloger would shoot Arthur, unless somebody stopped him.

"Don't just stand there. Give me a hand. If you don't, I swear I'll haunt you. You and yours will have my curse."

Oliver stepped on Rackley's fingers. When he still held on, he ground his heel into his knuckles. Finally, Rackley screamed and let go. His body could be heard bouncing as it hit the welter of ropes and battens holding up the sky drop.

Breathing hard, Oliver retrieved his handgun and climbed the ladder propped against the wall under the exit to the roof. The noise outside was now a steady, unrelenting roar of huzzahs. The martial strains of the band heading the parade were equally loud. Even now Gloger might be taking aim at Arthur.

Oliver became aware that his leg was sticky with blood where Griff's bullet had grazed him. He'd been so focused on taking Rackley out of action that he only now became aware of the stinging pain on his thigh. For a second his vision swam. Blinking to clear it, he took a deep breath and shoved at the trap door. It was heavy and for an agonizing moment resisted his efforts. Then it gave way and fell back on the roof with a crash.

The head of the colunmn had just rounded the corner from Water Street onto Holiday. President Arthur and the rest of the presidential party, including Mayor Whyte, General Sherman and ex-Mayor Latrobe stood in a row on City Hall's portico, prime targets.

Ladies below waved flags or handkerchiefs. Men threw up their hats. A roar exploded from their throats as the band struck up "Hail to the Chief."

Gloger, who'd been lying flat on the roof, saw Oliver. He had the barrel of McKinney's Sharps single-shot resting on a chimney pot. Probably, he'd already been sited on Arthur and about to pull the trigger when he'd heard the trap door falling open behind him.

He swung the gun around and fired just as Oliver dropped

and squeezed off a bullet from his Colt. Something hot creased his scalp. At the same time, Gloger flinched and Oliver knew he'd hit his shoulder. With a curse drowned by the noise exploding around them, Gloger rolled behind a collection of chimney pots. Even with a wounded shoulder, it would take him only seconds to reload. Oliver sprang around the barrier, yanked the weapon out of his hands and threw it over the parapet.

Baring his teeth, Gloger came at Oliver, hands outstretched. As he prepared to defend himself, he heard the crack of a bullet from the roof of City Hall.

CHAPTER THIRTY-NINE

"**Y**ou're damned lucky my man hit the right shooter."

"That's the fourth time you've said that, Harry." Despite his weary tone, Oliver was very glad that Waring, the sniper Harry Barnett had stationed atop City Hall, had managed to plug Gloger.

Now, he and Harry were racing down Charles Street. As the wheels of their barouche bounced over a raised cobblestone, Harry shouted at their driver. "Have a care! I've got a wounded man here." He shook his head. "Ollie, you belong in a doctor's office, getting that leg of yours looked at."

It's just a nick. He leaned his head against the cushions and closed his eyes. The dried blood caked below his knee pulled at his skin. An improvised bandage had stopped any further flow of blood. "First you have to take me home. I have to know that Chloe is all right."

He hadn't yet told Harry about Griff's role in the abortive plot to assassinate Arthur. Harry had ascertained, however, that Rackley was dead, as was McKinney. His City Hall sniper had picked off Gloger with a bullet to the brain. Miraculously, all of this had happened without Arthur, or any of the crowds cheering for him and the marching veterans being any the wiser.

"And that's the way we'll keep it, if we can," Harry declared. "The less that gets out about this nasty business, the better."

As the vehicle rolled up Madison, Oliver stared at the passing houses anxiously. He did not believe that Griff would harm

Chloe or Mrs. Milawney, but there was a lot about Griff that he wouldn't have believed until this day.

His fears were magnified when he saw several neighbors milling and whispering in front of the gate closing off the small alley leading to his garden.

"God in heaven," he whispered. Before Harry could stop him, he clambered out of the still moving carriage and limped across the street. "What's happened," he demanded as he pushed his way past two elderly women blocking access to the gate.

"Something terrible is going on in there. We heard screaming and a shot."

He tore the gate open and hobbled through. Then he heard it, the terrible, agonized weeping.

Heart pounding, he dragged himself past the maple which obscured his view of the back of the garden. Who was crying? It wasn't Mrs. Milawney. That wasn't her voice. Nor was it Chloe's. But whoever was making that dreadful noise sounded as if she'd had the heart torn from her.

Harry grabbed his shoulder. "For the love of heaven, Ollie!"

He lurched forward and then stopped, turned to stone by the grotesque tableau at the end of the garden. Felicia Rubman lay on the ground, her knees drawn up to her chin, her hair loose and her face buried in her hands. It was she whose wails reverberated in the hot stillness.

Beyond her, Cyrus Roe slumped against the back fence. He was pale and hatless. Blood from a wounded shoulder oozed through the linen material of his light-colored box jacket. Hannah Kinchman stood between him and Felicia Rubman. With one arm, Hannah sheltered Chloe against her skirts. With the other she trained a handgun on Roe.

Hannah took her eyes off Roe just long enough to shoot Oliver and Harry Barnett a brief, anxious glance.

"Thank God you've come. Chloe's fine," she said. "It was this young man who killed Dexter Rubman and who helped kill Enoch Rubman and the others. If I'm not mistaken, I believe he's ready to confess everything to you now.

"How much more of this can you take?" Harry demanded. He pointed at Oliver's leg where blood stained the outside of his pants.

"If there'd been time, I would have changed. But I fear there isn't time."

After hearing Cyrus Roe's garbled confession, Harry had turned him over to one of his men for safekeeping. He'd tried to persuade Oliver to see a doctor, but he had insisted on finding Griff first. With a sigh, Harry had agreed to drive him to Zephyrus while Hannah had stayed with Chloe and Felicia Rubman.

"What makes you think you'll find your cousin at home?"

"After he left the Holiday Street Theater, he never came to my house looking for the Remington-Beals. Where else would he have gone but home? I think Zephyrus is the only place in the world where he feels safe."

"So he's a rabbit diving for a bolt hole. Why are you in such an all-fired hurry to track him down?" Harry flicked his horse's rump with the whip.

"I'm afraid of what he might do. By now he must know that Arthur wasn't shot and that the plan to assassinate him fell through." Oliver stared at the houses flashing by. It was no use trying to protect Griff now. Cyrus Roe had implicated him too deeply.

"Did you suspect your cousin might be involved in the train accident?" Harry asked.

"I was beginning to. I learned that Ben Magruder went to see Griff after reading that article he published in the SUN. I believe Magruder must have threatened him."

"You mean threatened to beat him up or kill him?"

"Maybe. Maybe Magruder knew something about Griff's Point Lookout days, something that gave him power."

"Such as?"

Oliver turned away from Harry's expectant gaze. He wasn't

ready to put his worst doubts into words. Since that night at Kernans he'd suspected that Griff had escaped from Point Lookout by betraying his comrades so that Magruder could lay a trap for them. "I have no proof that Magruder threatened Griff, but when I learned that Enoch Rubman had been part of this Rivers and Harbors scheme, I knew all these strands had to be a connected in some way. I just didn't know what it was."

"And all the time the connection was Cyrus Roe," Harry mused. "He read the SUN article, then recognized Magruder on the train and followed him to your cousin's house. Afterward, he went to your cousin with his story about what Magruder, Nutwell and Rubman had done to his brother and sister. Singleton had his own reasons for wanting Magruder and Rubman out of the way, so he and Roe began to scheme."

Oliver nodded. "Griff must have known about Rubman's plans to be in that private car with Magruder and Nutwell. Roe would have known enough about the workings of the railroad so that together they could engineer the accident."

"Why do you think your cousin hated Rubman so much?" Harry asked. "Do you think it had something to do with this Rivers and Harbors scheme? Do you think Rubman objected to the idea of assassinating Arthur?"

"Possibly." Oliver kept his head turned, looking blindly at the trees and fields lining either side of the road. It could have been business matters, of course. But Oliver suspected that Griff's hatred of Enoch Rubman had been more personal. In the garden a few minutes earlier Hannah Kinchman had taken him aside and told him something that confirmed his suspicions. While she'd been pilfering Flora Penrose's medical records from Doctor LeSane, she'd seen Laura Singleton's name on a file and snatched that, too.

LeSane had prescribed nitrate of silver for Laura. She, too, had been diagnosed with syphilis. Had she, like Flora, been seduced by Enoch Rubman? Had he passed his disease to her? LeSane might not have even told Laura what she had. Instead, he might have gone directly to Griff with the information. Had

Rubman given his disease to his wife as well? Was that why poor little Felicia Rubman's child had been stillborn?

The pony cart pulled up in front of Zephyrus. "Do you want me to go in with you?" Harry asked.

"This is something I need to do alone."

After he dragged himself up the steps, he leaned for a moment on one of the columns supporting the portico. His leg had stiffened painfully.

Laura threw open the door. "Oh my Lord! What's happened to you? You're covered in blood!"

"Laura, is Griff at home? I must speak to him."

"He rushed in here wearing a Union uniform and looking just awful. When I tried to speak to him, he brushed me away and locked himself in his library. What's happened? I know something dreadful has happened. It's days now since he's acted like himself."

"Did he say anything?"

"He wouldn't speak to me. When I knock, he doesn't answer." Laura twisted her hands together. She looked distraught, her hair disheveled. "You must tell me what's going on! You haven't told him what I. . ."

"No, of course not. I haven't said a word. That's all forgotten." He pushed past her and hurried down the center hall to the library. He pounded on the paneled door. "Griff, it's Oliver. Let me in."

When Griff didn't answer, he tried the handle and then put his shoulder to the wood and shoved. The door was stoutly made. It didn't give easily. But finally the wood around the lock splintered and the door burst open. The library was empty. The window looking out on the gardens was open, its lace curtain blowing gently in the hot summer breezes.

Shoving the curtain aside, he climbed through the ground floor window and let himself down. As his feet touched the grassy ground below he heard a gunshot.

At first he thought someone might have shot at him. But after a moment, he realized that was not the case. The heart within him seemed to shrivel. He hurried as best he could down the swell of ground leading to the spot where Griff liked to sit. He rounded a stand of thick green yew knowing what he would find.

Griff sat in his wooden chair. He had changed out of his Union disguise and wore one of his fine white linen suits. He also wore his dark glasses. A gun lay on the grass next to the chair. Griff had used it to blow the top of his skull away.

CHAPTER FORTY

Police swarmed around Monument National. Their wagons blocked off the street where officers carrying truncheons stood guard. Crowds pressed around the barrier. Women stood on tiptoe and men craned their necks trying to get a look inside the bank doors.

"I hear they robbed it the night before President Arthur came to town," one woman in a beribboned bonnet informed another. "The bank was closed for the parade, so nobody was the wiser until this morning."

"Oh dear! I wonder how much money they got."

"No telling. I'm glad I didn't have my money in that bank!"

Oliver and Hannah looked at each other. "Why do you look so amused?" she inquired.

"Because I know who did have money in that bank. Rackley and his co-conspirators. I also think I know who emptied Bailey's vaults and how. I'll wager the thieves tunneled into them from the wine shop next door."

Hannah's eyes widened. "If you know so much about the thieves, why aren't you going to the police with your information?"

"Oh," Oliver said, taking her arm and leading her away from the throng, "I'll tell the authorities all I know when they come asking. Until then, let them figure it out for themselves."

It was the morning after Griff Singleton's suicide. Hannah had kindly spent the night with Chloe while Oliver had stayed at Zephyrus to console Laura and take care of the other arrangements necessary. Through her tears, she had confirmed what he already suspected. She had contracted syphilis from Enoch Rubman and Griff had discovered it. "I'll never forgive myself," she'd whispered. "Never!"

Now Oliver was escorting Hannah Kinchman back from Mrs. Battaile's where she had picked up her luggage. Hannah had agreed to stay on taking care of Chloe until Mrs. Milawney returned from nursing her nephew. Hannah would have to remain in Baltimore for a time, anyway, to give her testimony about Cyrus Roe.

"If you are concerned about the propriety of the arrangement," Oliver had told her, "I will sleep at the YMCA until Mrs. Milawney comes back."

Hannah had laughed at that. "I'm not worried about propriety. As a former actress and artist's model, I have no reputation to protect. Besides, you and I are not attracted to each other romantically. There's no possibility of impropriety in our residing in the same house for a few days."

Oliver glanced down at the top of her head. He admired and respected Hannah now. How could he do otherwise? After all, through her courage and resourcefulness she had saved Chloe from Cyrus Roe and forced a confession from that confused and vindictive young man. Few women would have had the daring to pluck a derringer out of a doll's grave and shoot the gun from Roe's hand. Hannah had done precisely that, then seized Roe's own gun and held him at bay while she cajoled him into confessing.

"Besides," Hannah continued, "we are both in mourning, you for your cousin and I..."

Her voice broke and Oliver stared at her curiously. Through her downcast lashes, he detected a suspicious glitter. "You are not still grieving for your brother. He's been released in good health, so I hear. So you must be in mourning for Beacher Penrose."

Silently, Hannah nodded. Above her high ruffled collar, her throat worked. "He and his wife were innocent victims in all this, really. By preying upon Flora, Enoch Rubman killed Beacher, too."

"You cared for him, didn't you?"

"How could one not care for a being so sensitive and talented? He was really too good for this world."

Or too weak for it, Oliver thought. But he didn't put that sentiment into words. Instead, he said, "When you first came to me you requested that I hire you to work as a detective."

"Yes, and you refused me. You said you had no interest in opening a private detecting agency."

Oliver squinted down the empty street and said carefully, "That was true then. I came to Baltimore to change my life. I thought I'd like to go into a more respectable business. But these last days have taught me something."

"About what?" Hannah shot him a curious look.

"About business and respectability, and about myself, I suppose." They had reached the house on Madison Street. Oliver paused in front of his steps to look into Hannah's questioning face. "My friend Harry Barnett once told me I couldn't change my stripes. He was right. I intend to open my own private detection business here in Baltimore. If you'd still like to work for me, I'll be very pleased to employ you."

Before Hannah could answer, the door was thrown open and the young woman Oliver had hired to stay with Chloe while they went to retrieve Hannah's things stuck her head out. "Oh, sir, you've received a telegram."

"Indeed? Then I'd better have a look at it."

But she had already run down the steps and thrust the telegram into his hand. He opened it and read the contents. A slow smile broke over his face.

"Good news?" Hannah inquired.

Not for Edson Bailey's bank. It's from a couple of friends of mine named Jake Jaggard and Danny Coy. The message is a simple one. 'Bon Voyage.' They've sailed for Europe this morning. By now they're on the high seas. And unless I miss my guess, I wouldn't be surprised if their bags are packed with stolen gold and Coy has his beautiful Maureen at his side dressed like a queen."

# # #

Prologue

Baltimore 1882

BERTRAM WALKED UNCERTAINLY on the drizzle-slicked wharf. Apple cores, fish leavings, rotted wood and other garbage slopped against the hulls of bugeyes, clippers, and skipjacks. Bertram couldn't hear their hemp lines creaking against the mossy pilings as they strained upward with the incoming tide. But he could feel the vibrations beneath his feet.

There were other vibrations—the steady thud of carts rolling past loaded with dry goods, the rap of feet as Negro oystermen came off vessels carrying baskets of shellfish and racks of canvasback ducks.

He tried to stop one of the sailors. The man, a grizzled individual with a knit cap pulled low over his forehead, paused. Bertram saw his reflection in the man's eyes—a slight boy, expensively dressed in woolen knickers, stockings, a shirt and jacket.

The clothes were rumpled. He hadn't succeeded in brushing away the bits of straw from the farmer's cart in which he'd sneaked a ride into town. He knew very well that he looked out of place. His outfit was not what a cabin boy might wear. But he'd had nothing more appropriate.

He wanted to explain all of this to the man staring down at him with an expression that was half-annoyed, half-curious. Yet all he could do was point at the clipper with tallest mast and then at himself. He took a square of paper from his pocket, unfolded it and handed it to the man. *The block letters on the paper read: My name is Bertram. I am deaf. I would like to go away to sea as a cabin boy. Please help me.*

Made in United States
Orlando, FL
29 March 2022

16268620R00129